Soul Echo: Discovery

By Lisa Stapleton

Soul Echo: Discovery

Published by Lisa Stapleton through Kindle Direct Publishing

Copyright © 2017 Lisa Stapleton

Cover Photo by Hudson Hintze of unsplash.com

Cover Design by Lisa Stapleton

M.
Thank you for reigniting my passion for this story and encouraging me to finish it and for everyone else that supported me through this process. It's only taken me ten years.
Hopefully the next one won't take as long…

Dr Andrew Hunter
1937

Shoving back the sleeve of his tweed jacket, Andrew looked at his watch for the umpteenth time and sighed. Fifteen minutes and counting. That was how long ago his meeting with the Governor should have started and with each passing minute, he was growing more and more impatient. Sure, he understood that sometimes meetings overran, or that traffic was unpredictable and could hold you up. What he didn't understand, however, was the lack of common courtesy. How hard was it to pick up a phone and call ahead to let them know that they were running a few minutes late? Andrew felt a pit of worry start to form in his stomach, were they intentionally running late to send him a message? No. Surely not.

Shaking his sleeve back down, he clasped his hands behind his back and resumed his pacing.

"Andrew sit down, you're going to wear out your soles." Richard teased, trying to lighten the mood a little.

Andrew scoffed, "Well, I can bloody well bill them for a new pair." Without missing a step as his assistant started to go through the notecards for the billionth time. Andrew had laughed at him when Richard had gone through and highlighted the first word on each card, insisting that this method would help Andrew to memorise them. To his credit, and Andrew's annoyance, the idea had actually worked, and he'd been forced to eat his words and apologise.

"You can wipe that stupid grin off your face as well, Richard." Andrew grumbled as he caught the smirk before Richard could hide it.

5

"And stop fiddling with the cards, too. If they're in the wrong order and you make me look a fool in the meeting, I'll have you on clean up patrol down in the animal lab for the rest of the week."

"Sorry." Richard mumbled, hastily ensuring the notecards were still in the right order. Andrew had sent Richard down to the animal lab once before when he'd been particularly annoying and he'd had an awful time of it. He'd come back complaining about the number of times he'd been shat on and Andrew had laughed and asked if he'd learned his lesson.

The closer the minute hand on the clock got to reaching the hour mark, the more frustrated Andrew became. This meeting had taken him months to set up and now it looked as though it wasn't even going to happen! Ridiculous! Andrew had heard rumours that the Ministry thought that his research was a waste of time, money and office space but he'd always assumed that they were just that. Rumours spread by lesser scientists. Now, as he paced back and forth, he was starting to worry that those rumours had some credence to them.

The door to the tiny, bland waiting room opened and Andrew looked up hoping not to see that blasted woman coming to make yet another excuse for the Governor. His eyes narrowed when he saw that it was her, and she stopped in her tracks as they made eye contact.

"Is he here?" Andrew demanded.

"No." She told them, taking a half step back in case Andrew started yelling. His reputation for being impatient was well known throughout the ministry's secretarial staff and they all dreaded being the ones to have to put up with him. A fact that he was well aware of and he did nothing to try and resolve it.

"I came to ask if you gentlemen would like a drink?" Her gaze very pointedly moved to Richard when she emphasized the word gentlemen and Andrew shook his head.

"So he's going to be a while then?"

"I could use a coffee, actually. White. Two sugars?" Richard said – ever the pacifist. Andrew rolled his eyes and sighed audibly. Richard was going to have to grow a backbone if he didn't want to end up being replaced.

"Anything for you Doctor Hunter?" Oh, was she still here? Andrew turned back to her with a bored expression.

"Black coffee." He'd barely finished speaking before she was out of the door leaving the two of them alone, and waiting once more.

Fifteen minutes later when the door reopened, Andrew turned and his expression quickly soured when he saw that the secretary's hands were empty.

"Does everything have a waiting list around here?" He demanded. Her eyes opened wide at his tone, and if he wasn't mistaken, her lower lip started to tremble.

"My apologies Dr. Hunter, but Governor Johnson is ready to receive you now. Your drinks are in the conference room also."

Grumbling under his breath, Andrew followed the secretary from the small room without checking to make sure that Richard was behind him – he knew better than to fall behind. She led the two of them down a winding corridor and through a large wooden door. Andrew passed through it following the secretary and trying to repel the sense of foreboding he felt as he crossed the threshold.

The conference room was large, with floor-to-ceiling windows that showed an almost perfect view of London between the blinds. Most of the room was taken up by an extravagantly large table, at which sat three men. The man in the centre rose immediately and came around to greet the two scientists. Portly, greying and red-nosed, he cleared his throat and waited for the secretary to let herself out and close the door.

"Dr Hunter, welcome!" The man beamed, though the smile went no further than his jowls, which wobbled as he spoke.

"Governor Johnson." Andrew stepped forwards and shook his hand, causing further movement in Johnson's jowls. At least if today went down the pan, he'd have those mental images to cheer him up a

7

bit. "A pleasure." Taking a step to the side, Andrew motioned to his assistant. "This is Dr Richard Cole, my associate."

The Governor nodded, and grasped Richard's hand much more briefly than he had held on to Andrew's. No sooner had he released Richard than he had gone back to his seat, though he remained standing.

"These are my consultants." He smiled. "Dr Iain Ashbury, Head of Research at the London Institute of Science, and this," He motioned to the other man, "Is Jim Michaels, an investor. We have looked over the information you sent us and we are ready to hear what you have to say."

Andrew nodded to each of the men as they were introduced before turning away to take his seat at the table, clearly indicated by the presence of the two coffee mugs. Richard was busy arranging everything on the table, setting up the projector and placing the notecards in front of Andrew ready for him to begin his presentation.

"Are we ready to start yet, Richard?" Andrew hissed as Richard busied himself about around him.

"Just a second, Dr Hunter."

While he waited, he reached for the mug in front of him and sighed. Milk and probably sugar. Peering into the other mug, he found it much the same and made a face. Today was going to be a long day.

"Ready when you are, Dr H." Richard murmured behind him. He sounded sympathetic, but Andrew would have him later about the casual use of his nickname in such a place. Grateful for a reason to put down the dreadful coffee, Andrew did so, placing it back on the table and picking up his note cards.

"If you gentlemen are sitting comfortably, I would like to begin now." Clearing his throat, Andrew began his presentation. "We have come here today to bring your attention to a fast approaching crisis." Andrew had made Richard go through this with him so many times that the boy no longer needed cues to know when to switch slides and he pressed the first button right on time, as words sprang up on the screen.

OVER POPULATION CRISIS PENDING

He waited a moment to let the information sink in before continuing, a bar chart replacing the words on the screen. "Our research shows that in the last fifty years alone, the world's population has increased by almost fifty percent. Based on this current growth trend, predictions show that the population will increase to a staggering six billion, four hundred million by the year two thousand and four, and that by the year two thousand and fifty the global population will be at the breaking point of eight billion, nine hundred million people.

"Early simulations show that this will be much more than the Earth can handle, and we should start taking the appropriate measures *now* to ensure the safe future of the Earth and the Human race."

Throughout the presentation, Johnson and his cronies had been muttering amongst themselves, and taking notes. Now, the three of them turned to face Andrew.

"And what measures are you proposing should be taken?" Johnson asked.

"I believe we should take control of the reproduction rates as soon as possible. Implement a system whereby couples are limited in the number of children they can have. Issue a licence for people that wish to try, even. We believe this will dramatically reduce the amount of teenage and accidental pregnancies. Especially if it is made a punishable offence."

"So you want to effectively put a cap on who can have sex and when?" Dr Ashbury asked. He had a gravelly voice – probably a smoker. "You can't do this to people, there will be riots."

"No, no. It's nothing like that. We're not trying to stop people copulating. They are perfectly able to do that as often as they like. What we need to control is the pregnancies."

"And what of the thousands of women who fall pregnant by accident every year? Are you going to force them to have an abortion?" Andrew opened his mouth to reply, but Ashbury continued to rail at him. "I suppose that next month you'll be back in here telling us that the senior citizens have to go. Anyone over a certain age should be put out of their misery, eh? What about the terminally ill? Shall we just euthanise the lot of them? I think you've been reading too much Science Fiction, Sir!" Ashbury was starting to go red in the face until Governor Johnson put a hand on his arm to silence him.

"I've heard enough." He spoke authoritatively, his jowls shaking as he looked between Andrew and Ashbury. "From both parties. This is obviously something that will take a lot of consideration. Very careful consideration at that. This meeting is adjourned for today. Dr Hunter thank you for coming. We'll be in contact." Johnson rose from his chair with a grunt and paused at the end of the table to shake Andrew's hand once more before leaving the room with the two consultants at his heels like trained dogs. Though Ashbury's face was solemn, Andrew could see the anger from before simmering beneath the surface and he certainly felt it in the tight grip of Ashbury's hand as he passed him.

"Well, that went well."

"Shut up, Richard."

"Yes sir."

Dr Richard Cole
1937

The ride back from the Governer's office was a long one. Not because of the distance they had to cover, but rather the fact that it was so uncomfortably quiet. Andrew had scarcely said three words to him since they had gotten into the car. From the look on his face, he was deep in thought and would be for the rest of the day, analysing the meeting and rethinking everything.

Richard gave up trying to make conversation and instead focussed on the drive back to the lab. It didn't take too long, and thankfully there wasn't a lot of traffic, and Richard gave a sigh of relief as they pulled into the car park. The silence would be over soon.

"Maybe Ashbury was on to something." Andrew mumbled, probably to himself but loud enough for Richard to catch it.

"Pardon?" He asked, turning to look at his boss.

Andrew looked away from the window now, turning to speak to him. He had that look on his face that he got when he had an idea. "Controlled sex. What if we could do it? What if we could program people to only be receptive to one partner? Complete human monogamy."

"You mean like animal monogamy?" Richard asked, raising his eyebrows. Andrew was definitely on to something here.

"Not quite. This would have to be different. Even monogamous animals will have a fling every now and then. I'm proposing only being able to be sexually active with one partner and non-receptive to everyone else."

"But that's impossible, right?"

"Richard, my dear boy. Nothing is impossible. Science will find a way. Come, I'll share my ideas with you and the rest of the team."

Andrew smiled and nodded, undoing his seatbelt and reaching for the door. He couldn't wait to hear this, to maybe actually be included rather than just run labs and get results for Andrew. Slamming the car door a little enthusiastically, he rushed to the boot to retrieve all of his equipment and hurried after his mentor. Maybe this would be the experiment that would finally raise him above the level of assistant.

Project Population Control
(P. P. C.)
Timeline of Events

1937 Scientists predict: Earth will be over-populated within the next 200 years if the birth rate cannot be controlled.

Claim is dismissed.

1941 A team of scientists in the UK start work on a microchip implant to control sexual activity.

1945 Preliminary trials begin using Primates.

1946 Primate results are promising. Negotiations begin to start human trials.

Protests begin after research is leaked to the press.

1947 An orphaned baby boy is chosen after human trials are given the go-ahead.

Experiment 01 begins.

1948 A protester breaks into the research facility and attempts to the steal the baby.

Press nicknames the baby '*Adam*'.

1949 3 more attempts are made to steal *Adam*.

Research facility moves to a more secure location.

1962 First error found: *Adam* fails to hit puberty on schedule.

1967 *Adam* finally hits puberty at the age of 20. 5 years later than expected.

1968 *Adam* dies.

1968-1969 Retesting begins on the implant.

1971 New implant is ready for trials.

1972 Female subject is chosen and implant placed. *Experiment 02* begins. Nickname: *Eve*

1973 Scientists start testing '*Paired Implants*'.

1978 *Paired Implants* tested using Primate Subjects. Tests are successful.

1983 Plans are drawn up for a group experiment testing the *Paired Implants.*

1987 *Eve* hits puberty as planned.

1992 *Eve's* Implant is activated fully. Monogamy experiments start.

1993 Monogamy testing is successful.

1994 Group experiments move forwards – Search for 'Parents' starts.

1997 Willing parents are found for the *Paired Implant* group. Contracts are written up.

1998 Test subjects are selected for the *Paired Implant* group and assigned to parents.

1999 Protests begin when the project is leaked.

Subjects are placed in homes around the country to keep their identities safe.

2013 The 10 subjects hit puberty on schedule.

2018 Present Day.

Steve Kay

"Special delivery for uhh.." Steve glanced at the name on the letter quickly even though he'd checked it three times on his way to the door. "Mrs Maysh."

"That's me." The short, plump blonde who'd opened the door smiled up at him. Stuffing the letter under his arm, Steve reached for the scanner attached to his belt and tapped in the information before holding the letter in front of it and zapping the barcode. Honestly, what was wrong with a clipboard and a pen? But Hunter had wanted 'authenticity' after all, and so here he was playing Postman Bloody Pat.

"Sign here, please." He held out the stupid stylus thing for Mrs Maysh to sign on the screen. She did as he asked, and he returned the device to his belt before retrieving the letter from under his arm and handing it to her. "Have a good day!" He beamed, before turning on his heel and heading back to his fake postal van.

"You too!" He heard her call after him before retreating back into her house. Climbing behind the wheel, Steve opened the glovebox and pulled out his mobile, unlocking it and tapping the screen before bringing it to his ear.

"Viv. Yeah, it's Steve." He grunted, clearing his throat and using a deeper voice than the fake one he'd put on to answer the door. "I've just delivered the one in Hull." He paused to let Vivienne respond, pulling the clip-on tie from his shirt as he listened and throwing it onto the passenger seat. "Yeah that's me finished." He paused again to listen, pulling the sunshade down to examine himself in the mirror, running a hand through his combed hair to muss it up. That was better.

He had no idea what was in the envelopes he had delivered, and he didn't really care. He knew that Viv's boss paid well, so he did as he was told. Even if it meant pretending to be a bloody postman and travelling up and down the country.

"Yeah, no problem." He ended the call without so much as a goodbye and slipped the phone into the centre console before clipping on his seatbelt and starting the engine. He had a long way to go to get home

Grace Maysh

Closing the door on the postman, Grace headed back down the hallway to the kitchen, dropping the letter on the counter and going to the kettle to finish making the cup of tea she had started before the postman had knocked.

It was at that moment that the washing machine decided to announce that it was finished, singing its little tune that told her the washing was ready to come out. Leaving the tea bag to diffuse in the hot water, she unloaded the clean washing into the basket and took it out into the garden to hang it out on the line and then rounded up another load to put on. With two boys (three including her husband) it was a never-ending chore, and she didn't mind for the most part, but would it kill them to put their dirty pants in the washing baskets instead of leaving them on their bedroom floors. Oh what she would have done to have a girl. It was too late now, though.

With that load whirling away, it was the dishwasher's turn to finish, and so she quickly put all that away before realising she was hungry. And no wonder – it was almost three in the afternoon and she hadn't eaten anything since breakfast.

She remade the cup of tea and stuck some crumpets in the toaster, only remembering the letter when she sat down to eat them. Leaving her lunch on the dining table, she quickly retrieved it from the counter and sat back down. It seemed like an ordinary letter and she could see no reason for it having been delivered by special delivery in the first place. There were no postmarks or stamps on the envelope.

Just her name and address. There wasn't even a return address on the back.

Finishing one of the crumpets in three bites, Grace wiped her hands on her jeans and slipped a nail beneath the flap on the letter and tore it open. As she saw the bold header on the top of the letter, she reached for the golden cross hanging from a chain around her neck, gripping it tight until it bit into her fingers, her heart racing slightly and her breath catching in her throat.

HUNTER AND SAMPSON SCIENCE ENTERPRISES

Practically holding her breath, Grace unfolded the letter and quickly read through the rest of the message. Putting it down on the table carefully, as if it might bite her if she man-handled it, she pushed her chair back and rose from the table in a bit of a daze. Reaching for her cup of tea, she wanted to call her husband, but she wasn't sure what she would say right now. Tea would help. She'd think it over and then call him. Half way to the cup, however, she faltered and never made it. With a small squeak, Grace fell to the floor in a dead faint.

Jennifer Dillon

Staring into her cup of coffee, Jen leant back in her seat and sighed, shoulders slumping. Today she was going home for the first time in almost eight months. With her first year of university successfully completed and the summer holidays bearing down on her, she had (very) begrudgingly packed up her belongings and moved out of the dorm block she had called home.

Luckily, she lived, and travelled light. Something she had learnt quickly enough after the first half term holiday had come around and she had been annoyed to find out that none of her belongings could be left in her room because during the two-week holiday all of the rooms were going to be deep cleaned. This meant she'd been forced to phone her father for help and have him come and pick her up in the car.

It wouldn't have been so bad if it had just been the two of them. But no, her mother and her youngest sister had also insisted on coming along. The resulting drive back home had been horrible. With four of them in the car along with all of Jen's belongings she and her sister had been crammed in the back seat for the entire duration of the three-hour journey. Never again. Now she only took with her what she could carry in a wheeled suitcase or a backpack. That way, she could get the train home instead.

Her large suitcase wobbled against her leg, pulling her from her reverie as a woman with a bulky double pushchair entered the train station coffee shop and barged past where Jen was sitting. Putting her coffee down a bit too quickly and scalding her fingers, Jen shot forwards to steady the case, Jen scowled after the woman who hadn't even muttered so much as an apology.

"Don't mind me." She grumbled, her mood darkening as the woman chose a nearby table to park the pushchair by before going to the counter. As soon as its mother was out of sight, the small bundle in the pushchair began to kick and scream. Jen groaned. She was going to have to put up with enough of this when she finally got home and she didn't need to be subjected to it any earlier than necessary.

Downing the last of her coffee a bit too quickly, Jen's thoughts turned to home and what awaited her there. She had recently found out that her youngest sister was pregnant. Tamlyn was only sixteen, much too young to even want to think about children, in Jen's opinion. In almost equal measure to Jen's disapproval their mother seemed to delight in the idea of even more grandchildren. Jen's other sister Elizabeth had two children of her own; twins that had recently celebrated their second birthday. Elizabeth had also gotten herself pregnant at sixteen, and Jen was starting to wonder what kind of thoughts their mother was putting into her sister's heads whilst she was away.

Desperate to get away from the unhappy reminder that she would soon be back in a house full of screaming children, Jen grabbed her things and fled the coffee shop as fast as her wheeled suitcase would allow. Out on the busy forecourt, Jen quickly looked up at the departure board as the nasal voice of the tannoy announced the arrival of the train she wanted. What luck! Pulling her suitcase behind her, Jen quickly boarded and decided to stand in the corridor so that she could avoid having to pull her luggage through the busy, crowded carriages. Besides, she could always sit on the top of her suitcase. She'd done it before.

After a truly horrendous journey Jen was glad to be off the train and back out in the cool, fresh air. When boarding the train, she had unwisely chosen a corridor containing a very smelly toilet. And since train toilets were never nice smelling, that was saying a lot. For a while, she'd thought about digging her perfume out of her suitcase to try and mask the smell but that would just make a stinky situation a hell of a lot worse.

Now free, she ambled away from the train station at a leisurely pace, enjoying the city air and letting the commuters pass her on either side in their haste to get home. It didn't matter to Jen, she wasn't in a rush to get back to that noisy house. These were going to be her last moments of peace for at least a few days so she was dead set on enjoying them.

It took almost ten minutes to reach the crossing that would take her into the city centre and on to catch the bus up to her parent's house. As Jen approached the traffic lights, she saw a man in the middle of the road heading away from her. The crossing lights changed back to red, and Jen watched in disbelief as the man stopped and doubled back into the road. Talking animatedly on his phone, he hadn't noticed the lights change because he'd dropped something and turned back to get it.

With the traffic lights no longer holding them back, the cars started to move. Jen called out to the man, trying to get his attention. With his phone tucked between his shoulder and his ear, he was facing away from the traffic and Jen. She sped up, her suitcase wobbling dangerously behind her in protest as she rushed forwards.

Calling out to the man again, Jen urged him to get out of the road, to abandon whatever it was he had dropped and get to safety but he still showed no sign of having heard her. Time seemed to slow down as she saw a car approaching rapidly. Coming full speed around the corner, the driver hadn't seen the pedestrian in the road and by now it was too late to stop.

The driver pressed down on the horn, beeping frantically and braking sharply. Unthinking, Jen abandoned her suitcase and ran at the guy in the road. The man, having heard the beeping and finally realising that something was wrong had straightened up, and was looking in horror at the car barrelling down on him.

21

Jen hit him hard, pushing him out of the car's path and forcing him to drop the phone he had clung to so desperately before. As she pushed forwards, her foot slipped on whatever it was that the man had dropped and she stumbled. The world seemed to enter real time again as the car that had been beeping at the man collided with Jen. The world exploded into whiteness. White noise deafening her; white shock and pain blinding her. For what seemed like an age, she lay there in the white until everything started to fade. In the moment before everything faded completely, she thought she could hear someone talking to her.

Aaron Maysh

Aaron yawned and narrowly avoided slopping someone's leftover spaghetti onto his shoes as he scraped a plate into the large black bin beside the sink. All this week he'd been rota'd in for the late shift and his body had yet to catch up with his new hours. In addition to his new nocturnal activities he'd also been handed the kitchen duty because Doug was off sick. Again.

Normally it wasn't so bad, but the kitchen's industrial dishwasher had broken two days ago and they couldn't get an engineer out to fix it until tomorrow morning. This meant that Aaron faced another night of washing the dishes by hand. The previous night had resulted over twenty sinks full and extremely pruned fingertips; the marigolds had just kept filling with water, so he'd abandoned them after the first sink full. The kitchen's swinging door opened inwards, and to Aaron's dismay more pots were brought in by the runners.

"God, who did you piss off?" One of them laughed. Aaron chuckled as if it wasn't the fiftieth time he'd heard that same thing; he didn't recognise this runner, so he must be fairly new. It wasn't surprising considering the turnover rate The Man at Arms had. They went through at least two new employees a week. This guy would probably be no different.

"You'll get to do it too, if you're here long enough." Aaron shot back as the two runners disappeared back through the swinging door and into the main restaurant. He glanced up at the clock and was very happy to see that in another five minutes it would be time for his break.

Shoving his hands into the sink with renewed vigour, Aaron was eager to wash as many pots as he could before his break because he knew that by the time he got back in half an hour, the pile would have been added to. A lot. If it wasn't too busy out in the restaurant, perhaps one of the managers would put a spare runner on wash-up and Aaron could do something else. Yeah, and pigs might fly.

"I think tomorrow night we'll get you doing something other than washing pots." Aaron's manager, George announced suddenly, appearing from the direction of the back office. Aaron jumped, yelping as he sliced his hand with the sharp knife he had been cleaning.

"Are you alright?" George asked, rushing over and pulling Aaron's hand towards him. He'd managed to slice open the meat of his thumb and the wound was pouring with blood and soap suds from the sink.

Aaron paled, feeling sick at the sight of all the blood.

"I think I need the first aid kit." Aaron groaned, looking away from his hand and swallowing bile.

"I don't know," George replied, "I think you might have to go the hospital to get this looked at. It looks pretty deep."

Aaron's eyes widened, "No! I'll be alright. I'll just go home and get my mum to look at it. She used to be a nurse, she'll know what to do."

George shook his head. "I'm sorry Aaron but it's company policy. I'm going to have to take you to the hospital, I wouldn't feel right letting you go home like this." Telling Aaron to stay where he was, George nipped back into the office he'd come from. When he returned he was carrying the accident book and the first aid box.

"Just need to fill this in. and put some pressure on that cut then we'll be off to A&E." George smiled, while Aaron's heart sank. "Actually," He added, "I think it's probably better if we just go straight there, you're looking a little green. I can fill this in later."

Aaron got out of the passenger side of the car reluctantly, cradling his wounded hand against his chest. He slowly undid his seatbelt with his good hand and wished he could fashion it into an escape rope. Anything to avoid going into the hospital. He slammed the door shut, wincing at the noise, and his stomach began to coil into knots as George locked the car. There was no escape now.

With a whoosh, the automatic doors opened before them and it was as if they had stolen away Aaron's breath in the same movement. As he fought to claw it back, the smell of the hospital blind-sided him, making him heave, and the overbearing clinical smell of disinfectant blocked out everything else. He felt light headed, as if he might pass out at any moment, but forced himself to trudge after George to avoid being dragged along. His manager cast a concerned glance his way. Why wasn't being in the hospital bothering him? Oh right, because he wasn't the one with the gaping hole in his hand.

As they stood at the desk waiting to be seen by the receptionist, Aaron looked around and immediately regretted doing it. A&E was truly the place of nightmares; machinery and equipment littered the hallways. Sick people sat slumped in chairs in the waiting room, their skin grey and lifeless. And as his eyes followed a line of colour down one of the corridors, it seemed to twist and mutate, stretching off into the distance until he could no longer see where it led. Thankfully George did all the talking and they were sent to take a seat with the usual 'it shouldn't be long.'

24

Dropping into a chair in the waiting room, Aaron imagined the colour draining from his skin until he was of the same lifeless pallor as the long-term residents of this hospital. He would be nothing more than a zombie, constantly feeding off his IV drip. With each passing second the coils in his stomach seemed to be growing bigger, writhing like snakes in a pit.

Fifteen agonising minutes later, Aaron was about ready to run from the hospital screaming. George was still watching him out of the corner of his eye with a worried expression, as though Aaron might die at any moment.

"Still with us, Aaron?" He asked. Aaron nodded feebly and George narrowed his eyes. "What's the matter? You're not afraid of hospitals, are you?" When Aaron didn't answer George chuckled. "There's nothing to be scared of, you'll see."

Eventually Aaron's name was called, and they were taken to a cubicle so he was spared having to explain to George about his embarrassing childhood experiences with the hospital. Like the time his mother had taken him in for his vaccinations and his arm had swelled like a balloon after the injections. And all the weird dreams he'd had about being poked and prodded in a lab.

"Well now, uh, Aaron." A doctor came through the cubicle curtain checking his clipboard. "What seems to be the problem?" Aaron held out his hand and looked away as the doctor peeled back the bandage George had given him and inspected the kitchen knife's handiwork.

"Well now, that's nothing we can't fix. I'll have a nurse come stitch you up."

Aaron opened his mouth to protest, but the doctor had already turned on his heel and left the cubicle, his pen scratching against the clipboard as he made notes.

"Guess they're really busy tonight." George mused. "All these kitchen staff trying to get out of doing the dishes."

His jibe at Aaron went unheard because he'd looked down at his injured hand, not realising the doctor had left the bandage peeled back and the wound was right there in plain sight. Red and raw and disgusting. His stomach did a back flip as he looked at it, so to prevent himself from vomiting, he looked at the curtain in front of him instead.

Almost instantly, a nurse entered the cubicle. She was tall, with hour glass curves and lips as full as her bust, her hair pulled up onto the top of her head in a messy bun, and if Aaron wasn't mistaken, there was a thermometer in there. Out of the corner of his eye, Aaron saw George sit up straight and grin. To his amusement, and George's absolute chagrin the nurse ignored him completely.

"Right, let's get you sorted out then." She smiled, batting her heavy-lidded eyes at Aaron, who nodded numbly and tried to avoid looking at anything vaguely hospital related. "Would you like some anaesthetic before I do the stitches?" She asked. Aaron looked up at her with wide eyes.

"Is it going to hurt?" He asked.

"It might sting a little." She told him.

"Can I try without?" Aaron asked. "I don't like needles."

The nurses nodded and smiled. "Of course."

"So how did you manage this then?" She asked him as she pulled on a pair of pink gloves before carefully peeled back the rest of the bandage. Aaron bit his lip to stop from wincing and looked up at the ceiling.

"I lost a fight with a kitchen knife. It was his fault." Aaron pointed a thumb at George with his good hand.

"That wasn't very nice of him, now was it?" The nurse chuckled, she was very nice and obviously trying to distract Aaron and make him feel calmer. It was a wasted effort. "Where do you work?"

"At a restaurant." Aaron replied, "The dishwasher broke."

"You should stop by for a bite to eat sometime." George added, winking.

The nurse ignored him, instead focusing on Aaron's injured hand. With practiced movements, she opened a suture pack and deftly sewed his wound closed. When she was done, she gave it a quick clean with an antiseptic wipe, causing Aaron to release a sharp hiss, before putting a large plaster over the stitches.

"Oh, don't be a baby." George teased, laughing as Aaron shot him a glare.

"Thank you." Aaron smiled, turning to the nurse and rising from his seat to leave, holding his hand against his chest protectively again.

"Just a moment," The nurse trilled, "I can't let you leave just yet, I'm afraid." Aaron sank back into his chair. What torture was she going to inflict on him now? She rose from her seat, taking with her the tray that had all the gauze and sutures on, and ducked out of the cubicle. She returned less than a minute later with a sheet of folded paper, which she pressed into Aaron's hand.

"Instructions on how to clean your stitches. You be careful at work," She beamed, "Wouldn't want to see you in here again now, would we?" She winked, before vanishing through the curtain, no doubt off to sew up someone else. Aaron rose slowly from the bed and looked at the piece of paper in his hand, while George tried to hide a smirk behind his hand.

"What's so funny?" Aaron demanded, opening the piece of paper as they finally left the hospital, trying not to look at anyone they passed in case he saw something disgusting.

"That nurse was totally into you, and you completely ignored her."

"Don't be ridiculous."

"I'm telling you Aaron, you just missed out on a shot with her."

"George, do you even hear the stuff you say?" Aaron rolled his eyes and quickly scanned the instructions he'd been given for his stitches. It seemed simple enough. Keep it clean. Don't pull at the threads. Like he was going anywhere near that anyway. Reaching over,

George snatched the piece of paper from his hand, a smug grin plastered across his broad face.

"So, if she's not interested, what's her phone number doing on the bottom?"

Jennifer Dillon

As she woke up, Jen didn't realise where she was. Everything was too bright, and her head was pounding. Looking around, she saw her family around her. What were they doing in her bedroom, and why were they being so noisy? She tried to sit up, but a shooting pain in her left shoulder forced to lay back down again with a gasp.

"Jennifer, baby, you're awake!" She heard her mother exclaim.

"Where am I?" She asked, her throat was dry and it made her cough.

"Here you go sweetheart." Her mother rushed forwards to give her some water from a glass that had a straw in it. Why had she had it ready? What was going on.

"Ahh, I see she's finally awake." Jen looked round; she didn't recognise this man's voice. Her eyes widened when she saw him. He was tall, kind eyed and dark haired and was wearing the white coat of a doctor. Something clicked in her mind and she remembered what had happened; she'd been hit by a car!

"I'm Doctor Roland. Jennifer, can you tell me what happened?" He asked, moving closer to the bed and waiting for Jen to finish her drink.

She nodded and pulled away from the straw. "Jen. I was hit by a car." She croaked.

"That's right." Doctor Roland smiled, "I heard all about it from the man who brought you to the hospital. You did a very brave thing today, Jen."

"Can't have been very smart though, if I ended up in the hospital." Jen frowned. Doctor Roland ignored her comment.

"You've got a bit of a nasty bump to the head, and you've broken your left collar bone." He told her. "You'll be in pain for a little while, but other than that I think you were very lucky."

"Lucky?" Jen's father finally spoke up, she'd been anticipating him going off on one. "How is it lucky that she got by a car in the first place?"

"Please, Mr Dillon, I merely meant that she could have come out of this accident with much more severe injuries than a broken collar bone and a concussion."

"Who brought me in? What was his name?" Jen asked, hoping to defuse her father before he got too angry.

"It was a Mr. Ellison." Doctor Roland smiled down at her, "You probably saved his life today."

"What? That moron is here? Where is he? I want to have a few words with this Mr. Ellison." Jen's father jumped to his feet, his face turning red.

"He is no longer on the premises." Doctor Roland replied curtly, taking a step backwards. He looked down at his watch, "I'll come back to check on you in a little while, Jen, I think your family might want to spend some time with you before visiting hours are over."

Coward. Jen thought as she watched him retreat from the room as fast as he could. Why should he get to escape when she couldn't? As soon as he was gone, she turned to glare at her father.

"What are you looking at?" He demanded.

"Did you have to be so rude?"

"I wasn't being rude. I was just asking a question."

"Well he didn't get me hit by the car dad, I did that to myself." Jen sighed to herself as her father declared that he was going to get some coffee. She wondered how long the visiting hours were, and whether feigning sleep would get rid of her family faster. Probably not. She wasn't that lucky. The medically induced haze over her brain started to fade, and Jen realised that her sisters were also in the room. Elizabeth had brought her sons; two-year-old twins Danny and Jake, and now that the Doctor had fled the room, they started up the racket that had woken Jen in the first place; arguing over what to watch on their tablet. Danny apparently wanted Paw Patrol while Jake wanted Dinosaur Train. Both shows were annoying as hell and Jen hoped that they'd just play a game or something.

"Mum." She croaked.

"What is it honey?" Her mother was by her side instantly, which made Danny pout and start to throw a temper tantrum because Grandma wasn't paying him any attention anymore and Jake had gotten his way with the tablet.

"Everything hurts, can I get some more pain killers?"

"I'll go and find a nurse darling."

Jen regretted asking this, because as soon as her mother was out of the room, Jake joined Danny in his tantrum and the two of them were soon wailing the hospital down.

"Oh, for god sake. Now look what you've done." Elizabeth sighed, having to look up from her phone to try and calm her own children down. The horror.

"I didn't do anything!" Jen protested.

"Of course you didn't."

Their other sister, Tamlyn, quietly moved over to the twins and tried to pacify them. Whatever she was doing seemed to work, and they soon quietened down. She had probably bribed them with ice-cream or something else laden with sugar. Elizabeth went back to her phone and Tamlyn's attempts at calming the twins worked. But how long would it last?

Staring up at the ceiling, Jen decided that she would try feigning sleep after all.

Dr. Jeremy Hunter

Click, clack, click, scrape-

Jeremy grimaced as he heard the lopsided, heavy footed approach of his secretary Vivienne. Every other one of her steps produced a terrible scraping sound to go with the annoying click-clack of her stilettos on the tile flooring.

He often considered putting in carpet to stop the annoying sounds, but always decided against it when he realised it meant people would be able to approach his office without him hearing them coming.

He didn't like that idea. Not one bit.

Two sharp raps on the door signalled her arrival and Vivienne opened the office door without waiting for him to call her in. She knew well enough by now to just come in if there was nothing in his diary to say otherwise. He didn't even look up as she entered, instead he was leaning over his desk on one elbow, his hand shoved into his greying hair as he made notes about the project.

"Doctor Hunter, I've just received word that all ten of the letters have now been delivered." At least Vivienne had a pleasant enough voice. Not too high, not to nasally. Just right. Jeremy looked up at her and smiled.

"Thank you, Vivienne. Please get IT to start monitoring the website traffic straight away." She nodded and started to leave the room. A foot away from the door, she stopped and turned to face his desk again. He hated it when she lingered.

"Is there anything else I can get you before I go to lunch?" She asked politely.

Jeremy thought about it for a moment and peered into his coffee mug where the remnants of his previous coffee lingered. Staining the porcelain. Mocking him. The last mouthful always went cold before he got around to it, and he usually didn't realise until it was already in his mouth. The rest of the time it was spilt on his desk. Both were equally as annoying.

"Yes," He replied eventually, "I'll have another coffee and a ploughman's sandwich please, Vivienne." Jeremy hadn't eaten since, well, he couldn't actually remember the last time he'd eaten. Had it been yesterday? Or perhaps the day before? Nodding, Vivienne, left his office. Jeremy watched her go, listening to the click, clack, click, scrape of her walk and wondered why she didn't just buy a more comfortable pair of shoes.

Once she was out of earshot, Jeremy relaxed into his chair and brought up a new window on his computer. Of course he wanted IT to monitor the site, but he also wanted to monitor it himself. He wasn't very good at leaving things to other people. That's what his last girlfriend had told him anyway, though she hadn't said it quite so politely. There was no traffic on the site yet, but he'd expected that. The subjects had only just received their letters, they'd need time to process this new information. He doubted there'd be anyone that would rush to the site, but still, he wanted to see it when it did happen.

Now the experiment was finally beginning. His father's life work was now his and he couldn't wait.

Farrell Brennan

Farrell was in his bedroom avoiding his family. Ever since they'd received the letter about his implant they'd been walking on egg shells around him; afraid to say anything that might upset him and treating him like a child. In return, he kept up the appearances of a sulking child in order to be left alone with his thoughts.

This tactic, however, had turned against him after the first day. Left alone to his own thoughts, he found himself wallowing in old insecurities; nurturing his deep seeded suspicion that he was gay, no matter what the letter said. He'd never really been attracted to women (aside from Beyoncé, but everyone was attracted to her, weren't they?) and he'd always been a lot more comfortable around men than the opposite sex.

It had gotten to the point where he found it almost impossible to ever imagine himself being with a woman. Maybe it was just because he'd always felt so awkward around women, and it had formed a vicious circle; he never approached women because of his awkwardness, and women had stopped approaching him because of his lack of interest.

The thought that he had a partner out there somewhere was unnerving. He felt like he was supposed to be living up to the expectations of someone he hadn't even met yet. The letter had come with a website link, and it had made it very clear that all of the pairs were male-female. A part of him wanted to rebel against this expectation; maybe if he could find out if he was straight one way or another he could be content in continuing in this experiment that had been forced upon him.

He opened the link to the website a while ago but not actually looked at the site. Now he was distracted from his thoughts by a bleep from his computer announcing he'd received an instant message, Farrell turned away from the wall he'd been staring at and looked at the monitor. It was David. A witty, intelligent guy Farrell had met last week in MovieZone. He had short, side-swept black hair, blue eyes and they had bonded over a comedy film they both liked.

After a conversation that had somehow sucked away almost an hour, they had traded emails to IM each other and later; phone numbers. And there had been a lot of both IMs and texting. A couple of days after they had started talking, Farrell had found out that David was openly gay, and suspected that he was harbouring a growing attraction that Farrell wasn't been sure how to deal with, but was starting to consider exploring.

He smiled as the instant messaging window flashed within seconds of him sending his last message.

Davy: Up to much?
Farrell: Nah, just bored You?
Davy: Was thinking of going to MovieZone. If you're not doing anything, you're more than welcome to join me.

Farrell paused before replying. He'd been trying not to encourage David too much, for fear of giving him the wrong idea. But now he wasn't sure if he cared. Maybe he wouldn't be giving him the wrong idea at all. Maybe David could help him figure it all out.

Farrell: Sounds fun. Your place?
Davy: Yeah. Unless you want me to come over to yours?
Farrell: My parents have to be up early in morning, so yours it is lol.
Davy: Cool. Meet you at MZ in 15?

Farrell: See you there.

Farrell smiled and closed down his computer. Tonight would be a deciding moment in his life. The first fluttering of nerves twitched in the base of his stomach and he tried to ignore it, forcing himself to rise from his computer chair. After tonight he would either be certain of his sexuality or more confused than before. That's if David really was interested in him as more than just a friend. They hadn't really broached the subject properly, instead skirting around the issue because neither of them wanted to ruin whatever it was they had. Right now they could just be friends, but if something happened, who knows if they could ever go back to that? Farrell pushed away the negative feelings and tried to ignore them niggling at the back of his mind.

Grabbing his wallet and spraying on some cologne, Farrell went downstairs to leave a message for his parents. They were fine with him coming and going as he pleased, but they liked to know what time he would be back. He was unsure of what time to put this time around, so he left it vague, promising to phone if he would be staying out all night.

It took a little less than fifteen minutes to get to MovieZone, and by the time Farrell had arrived his nervousness had increased substantially. Rubbing his sweaty palms on the front of his jeans, Farrell paced in front of the store as he waited for David to arrive. With each passing second he became more and more sure that David wasn't actually going to turn up, and that this was some sort of a joke.

Finally, David appeared around a corner and Farrell's heart leapt and he sighed audibly with relief. Stepping forwards to greet him, he suddenly realised he wasn't sure whether he should just say hi, or go for a hug or something. In the end, he decided to hang back and see how David greeted him instead.

"Sorry I'm a little late." David smiled, opening his arms and embracing Farrell, who reciprocated. It was a short hug, but it was a good one, and Farrell breathed in the citrus fragrance of David's shampoo. It mingled pleasantly with his skin-warmed cologne.

"It's fine, I wasn't waiting long." Farrell reassured him as they stepped back from each other. "So what were you thinking of getting?"

"I'm not sure really, I was thinking of having a look at the new releases and seeing if anything tickled my fancy."

A little over twenty minutes later, the two of them left the store armed with an action film, a comedy, a rom-com that David had professed his undying love for; Farrell had never seen it so of course this had to be remedied, and a couple bags of popcorn. No movie night was complete without popcorn.

It was a quick walk back to David's apartment, and Farrell looked around it in awe. It was spacious, with an open plan living room and kitchen. On the far wall there was a large flat screen TV, and a handful of gaming consoles. The large sofa looked comfortable and boasted reclining seats at either end. The most impressive feature of the room, however, was a host of floor-to-ceiling dark oak shelving units filled to bursting with a large collection of books, films and video games.

"Wow, that's quite the collection." He headed toward it to have a closer look.

"Thanks, it took a lot of effort collecting all this, I'll tell you."

Farrell nodded; he could definitely appreciate how long it must have taken to amass such a collection. It made his three tiny shelves back home look like a barren wasteland.

"So, what should we watch first?" David asked. When Farrell shrugged, David closed his eyes, thrust his hand into the carrier bag and pulled one out. "Looks like we're watching the rom-com then!" He grinned mischievously.

"You peeked!" Farrell argued; pulling David's arm toward him and snatching away the DVD he had been holding up so triumphantly.

"I did not!" David laughed, "You didn't want to pick, so you must suffer the consequences!"

"Not if I hide the DVD!" Farrell grinned, before turning and running through one of the doors that led out of the living room. He slammed the door shut behind him, breathing heavily from the sudden exertion and looked around the room. He cursed to himself for having chosen the bathroom to hide in, and wondered where he could stash the DVD.

"You have to come out sometime!" David called through the closed door. With nowhere better to hide the DVD that didn't involve sticking it in the toilet, Farrell lifted his t-shirt and wedged it in his waistband. He opened the door with a triumphant grin and happily informed David that he could search all he liked.

While David disappeared into the bathroom to search, Farrell went quickly to the discarded carrier bag and dug out a different DVD. He tiptoed over to the TV and slipped it into the DVD player before heading over to the sofa and sitting carefully so the DVD case didn't stab him in the stomach.

"Alright, I give." David sighed, coming out of the bathroom to join Farrell on the sofa. "Just let me know where you've hidden it when you leave, or I'll never find it." Farrell nodded and settled back on the sofa with a smug grin while David fetched the popcorn.

As they sat there together, centimetres apart and sharing the bag of popcorn, Farrell felt almost as if there was an electric current bouncing between them both. He wondered if David could feel it too and chanced a surreptitious glance in his direction. He looked absolutely fine, watching the film intently and munching on popcorn. No obvious inner turmoil going on there. Perhaps it was just him then; he was probably just letting his imagination run wild with him.

Shifting in his seat, Farrell moved to get a handful of popcorn. He jumped when his fingers met David's warm hand rather than the popcorn they had both been reaching for and was glad that his darker skin made it hard to detect a blush.

"After you." He smiled.

"What a gentleman." David teased, sticking out his tongue and tossing a piece of popcorn toward him. Farrell tried to catch it in his mouth and failed spectacularly. The movement brought him a lot closer to David, almost closing the distance between them and for a second, he wasn't sure what to do.

Grabbing the fallen piece of popcorn, he lifted it to his mouth, watching as David swallowed nervously and leant forwards. This was it, the moment of truth. Farrell ate the piece of popcorn quickly; hoping to clear his mouth for what he thought was coming. His heart was thumping in anticipation and for a moment he wondered if it was so loud that David could hear it.

Closing the gap between them, Farrell pressed his lips to David's in what he hoped was came across as a gentle, exploratory motion rather than the desperate, confused one that it actually was. He kept his eyes open long enough to watch as David relaxed a little and closed his eyes.

Farrell did the same. He was inexperienced when it came to romance, and he was depending on David taking the lead; at the same time hoping fervently that he wasn't so terrible that David would laugh at him.

He felt a probing lick on his bottom lip, and opened his mouth, granting David entrance. As they kissed, he felt David's hands on his waist pulling him closer. He obliged, shuffling forwards a fraction when suddenly David's warm mouth and soft lips retreated from his own.

He opened his eyes, and found David holding up his t-shirt and smirking.

"So that's where you hid it." For a moment, Farrell was confused, until David grabbed the DVD case he'd stashed in his waistband.

"Oh, that." He smiled sheepishly. "I guess this means you win."

"Well, I guess I do." David grinned with a wicked gleam in his eye. He tossed the DVD case over the back of the sofa and gently pushed Farrell backwards against the sofa cushions. As he lay back, David leant down over him, and Farrell was swept away once more by David's intoxicating fragrance, and his soft, tender kisses. In the background, the action movie carried on unwatched, the only witness to Farrell's first truly romantic encounter. He'd had girlfriends before at

39

school because all his friends were doing it. None of their kisses had ever felt so amazing.

Jennifer Dillon

Jen lay in bed reading through a book from the hospital's tiny collection. It comprised mostly of books that had been left behind by visitors or patients. The one she had chosen was turning out to be a bit miserable, and she decided to put it down before she got any more depressed by it.

"She's just behind this curtain." Jen heard a nurse saying, and felt vaguely like she was in some kind of game show. What's behind curtain number one? She thought, with a half-hearted chuckle.

Visiting hours had ended hours ago, and Jen had been extremely glad when the nurse had come round to kick out her family. "Thank you." She had mouthed to the nurse when she'd dared to open her eyes and watch her family leave. The nurse had simply winked and pulled the curtain around the bed.

"Poor dear," She had said as she'd ushered Jen's mother away, "Must be exhausted."

Perhaps it was another doctor come to make sure that her collar bone was in the right position to set nicely, or the physiotherapist coming to remind her of the exercises she had to do to make sure she was still using her arm properly.

"Thank you." Jen heard a man reply, his voice sounded vaguely familiar, so maybe it was a doctor she had already seen today. She was toying with the idea of feigning sleep again. If it was a doctor and they found her awake, they'd be likely to poke her where it hurt.

It wasn't a doctor. It was a man with mousey brown hair, blue eyes and a kind face.

"You must be Jennifer." He smiled.

"Jen." She corrected.

"Sorry."

There was an awkward moment where neither of them said anything. Jen looked up at the man expectantly, and he ran a hand through his hair.

"My name's John. John Ellison."

Jen's eyes widened as she remembered where she had heard this name before. This was the man that she had pushed out of the way of the oncoming car. This was the idiot behind her being in hospital. He was lucky her dad wasn't still here.

"I thought visiting hours were over." She replied a little curtly.

"The nurse let me in."

"Why?"

"Bribery." John winked, and Jen wasn't sure whether he was telling the truth or not, she'd heard the nurse giggling, so maybe he was. Exactly what he'd bribed her with though, she'd rather not know. "I came to say thank you for today. And that I'm sorry you're in this condition because of me."

"Why didn't you get out of the road?" Jen demanded.

"I thought the crossing was still green."

"Didn't you hear me shouting you?"

John shook his head. "I was too busy talking on my phone."

"What was so important that you had to stop in the middle of the road for?"

John reached into his jacket and pulled out his wallet.

"You're going to bribe me now, too?" Jen narrowed her eyes.

"No." He pulled something small out of his wallet and held it out to Jen. "I dropped this."

Jen looked down at what he'd given her. It was a photograph of a beautiful black-haired woman. She had big, expressive green eyes and was laughing at whoever was taking the picture. She looked so happy and vibrant.

"Your wife?" Jen asked, offering the picture back to John. He nodded and took it. "She's very pretty."

"Thank you. This is the only photo I have left of her." He tucked the picture back into his wallet and put it safely in his back pocket. "She died." He continued, "In a fire. The rest of my pictures of her - of us - were lost at the same time."

"I'm very sorry for your loss."

Ok now Jen felt a little bad. She had been so angry after she'd woken up in the hospital with a broken collar bone, but now she felt herself feeling sorry for him. Now that she understood why he'd stayed to pick up the picture, she couldn't bring herself to hold it against him. If it had been the only picture left of someone she loved then she probably would have done the same.

Suddenly, John moved forwards and took Jen's good hand. "I'm really very sorry for what's happened to you because of me. If there's anything I can do for you - anything at all - you just let me know."

"Just promise me you'll be more careful on the roads." Jen smiled, before adding, "I'm not looking for compensation or anything like that. Though you might want to avoid my dad."

"I hope you'll forgive me, Jen. You really saved my life today."

"I really doubt the car would have killed you, but I forgive you."

"Never say never, Jen."

There was a rustling noise behind them and the friendly nurse from before poked her head around the curtain.

"I'm sorry Mr. Ellison, but I'm going to have to ask you to leave now."

John nodded to the nurse and removed his hand from Jen's. "I hope you get better soon." He smiled, "You're a great girl, Jen, not many people would have done
what you did for me."

"Try to get some proper sleep now, Jen. Before morning." The nurse smiled, before closing the curtain behind herself and John. She definitely needed to sleep before morning. There was no way she could face her family on no sleep. Jen could hear giggling again as the two of them walked off and suddenly Jen wasn't so sure she should believe the grieving widower story.

Aaron Maysh

George had given Aaron a lift home from the hospital to save him getting the bus - and partly because his managed was feeling a little guilty for having made the accident happen in the first place. Waving goodbye, Aaron slipped in quietly through the front door. It was late and his parents had already gone to bed. His father was a notoriously light sleeper and was always in a terrible mood if he didn't get enough sleep. He also didn't want his mother to wake up and start fussing over his injured hand. He wouldn't put it past her to take the dressing off and re-do it herself as soon as she saw it.

So far so good. He managed to avoid the creaky step as he ascended, and as his stomach rumbled loud enough to wake the dead, he cursed himself for not remembering he had not eaten yet today. Creeping back down the stairs he headed into the kitchen to see what was for tea. His mother would normally make him something and leave it in the fridge.

Aaron was quite capable of making food for himself, but his mum always made him food if he was out. She did the same for his brother Jesse. Sure enough, there was a plate covered in cling film on the top shelf, with an A drawn on it with the white board marker pen. Putting the plate on the table, he turned back to the fridge and grabbed the milk carton.

"Holy crap!" He nearly dropped the milk as he shut the door and revealed someone standing there. "Jesse how many times do I have to tell you don't do that to me!" His younger brother merely laughed and stole the milk out of his hand. "Hey!"

"Shh." Jesse smirked. "Or we'll wake dad up and you'll get into trouble again."

Aaron sighed. It was true. The last time Jesse had snuck up on him at night he had yelled out and dropped a jar of jam. The yell and resounding smash had brought his father downstairs pretty sharpish thinking that someone was breaking into the house. Aaron had been lectured on the finer points of silence being a virtue, whereas Jesse had quickly lied and told their father that Aaron had woken him as well. Jesse had then slipped off back to bed and left his brother to clean up the mess he'd caused.

Peeling the cling film from his plate, Aaron sat at the table and guarded his food from his brother. He wouldn't put it past Jesse to try and steal some – all he seemed to do was eat lately and whenever Aaron complained about the food theft to his mother, she would remind him that 'Jesse is a growing boy.'

"So how was work?" Jesse asked, his top lip covered in milk after swigging straight from the opened carton.

"Jesse that's disgusting." Aaron groaned, pulling a face, "Use a glass. And grab me one while you're at it." Jesse rolled his eyes but fetched the glasses anyway.

"Work was - eventful." Aaron raised his injured hand and carefully pulled back the bandage to show his brother.

"Now that's disgusting." Jesse laughed, "I bet you passed out, didn't you?"

"I Did not!"

"Uhuh, sure."

"Then how do you explain the nurse giving me her phone number?" Aaron challenged.

"Was she blind?" Jesse shot back, dodging away from the fork Aaron jabbed in his direction.

"How's your day been?" Aaron asked, deciding it would be safer to change the subject.

"It wasn't that bad till I got home from school." Jesse frowned.

"Why's that? Did Dad find out you've not been handing in your homework on time again?"

Jesse's expression turned dark, and he looked down at the table, picking at one of his thumbnails. After a moment he looked up and opened his mouth but a creak on the stairs stopped whatever he was going to say.

Instead he gave Aaron a quiet "No." and pulled the milk towards himself. Aaron waited a few moments to see whether Jesse was going to add anything to his no, or just leave it at that. Apparently, it was going to be the latter. After filling a glass with milk, Jesse rose from the table, mumbled "Night." And vanished back up the stairs. Frowning after him, Aaron made a mental note to try and ask his brother what had happened again tomorrow before pushing the thought from his mind and digging into his food.

Grace Maysh

Upstairs in bed, Grace couldn't sleep. Normally she'd be out like a light as soon as she and her husband Jeff had prayed. Their heads would hit the pillows and then that would be it until morning. But tonight she couldn't drift off. She had stared at her husband's still form for a while, listening to his breathing and watching the steady rise and fall of his chest in the vain hopes that it would act as some sort of hypnosis and pull her under. It hadn't.

After a while, she resorted to counting his breaths, and then sheep, but nothing seemed to be working. Ever so slowly, she rolled over and slid out of the bed. Digging around blindly for her slippers, she paused and held her breath as she heard something move beneath the bed. Jeff grumbled in his sleep but thankfully didn't wake.

Grace left her bedroom with every intention of going down to the kitchen and fixing herself some hot chocolate – it never failed to help her get to sleep, ever since she was little – but she paused on the top step when she heard voices in the kitchen.

Aaron must be home, she realised, but who was with him? She waited for the second person to talk again and gave a sigh of relief when she realised it was only Jesse.

"It wasn't that bad till I got home from school." She heard Jesse tell his brother and her breath hitched in her throat – was he going to tell Aaron about the letter? She'd begged him earlier to give them time to tell Aaron themselves, but would he keep his promise? Taking another step down she groaned as she hit the creaky step. Crap! How could she have forgotten? Pulling her foot back to the step above, she waited to hear what Jesse would tell his brother.

Moments passed, stretched out by the silence and she almost couldn't take it any longer, practically on the verge of going down there now and telling Aaron herself. Had Jesse replied in a whisper? Had the sound of her frantic heart beat drowned out the voices downstairs? When she heard the groan of a chair being pushed back she realised it was neither, Jesse wasn't going to say anything.

She heard him say goodnight to his older brother and had just enough time to hide in the shadows of the dark bathroom before Jesse appeared at the bottom of the stairs and came up to bed. Clutching the cross around her neck and praying he wouldn't come into the bathroom and find her there in the dark, she waited until she heard his door open and shut before daring to venture back out.

Sighing, she returned to the bedroom and slipped into bed beside her husband's sleeping form. There was no way she was going to be able to sleep now, but the alternative was going downstairs and having Aaron ask why Jesse was in such a bad mood about today. She couldn't handle that, not right this second. At least if she stayed in bed she would be able to put it off until morning.

"God help me." She whispered as she lay there, praying for the strength to get through tomorrow. When she finished the rest of her silent prayer, she remembered something that might help in the top drawer of her night stand. Pulling open the drawer carefully she drew out a white box – sleeping pills left over from years ago. Peeking at her husband out of the corner of her eye to make sure he was still sleeping, she pushed a pill through the foil cover and slipped it into her mouth. She placed the pills back in her draw and shut it carefully, wincing when the wood stuck and she had to give it a shove.

Laying back, she snuggled closer towards his warm body and waited for the pill to take effect. It didn't take long.

Aaron Maysh

Aaron woke early the next morning, exhausted from a fitful night of vivid and strange dreams. He'd been younger in his dreams – probably around four or five – and he was at a play park with his brother. He couldn't remember seeing his parents at first, but he and his brother were happy enough playing on the swings. Jesse had been in one of the baby swings with the back supports and leg holes so that little children wouldn't fall out. Aaron had been on one of the proper swings, and had been getting higher and higher as he showed off for his brother, his little legs pumping hard in his efforts.

Jesse had thought the whole thing was absolutely hilarious and was clapping his encouragement, and some other kids in the park told Aaron to jump so he had done it. Jumping right from the top of an arch, he had flown well, but his landing was off and he hit the gravel like a lead weight. The pain had been instant, a burning that ran the length of his shins and forearms, and then suddenly his mother was there.

She was picking him up and telling him it was okay. Hugging him close against her and accidentally pressing her hair into his face and telling him how she'd thought she would never see him again – and suddenly it was not his mother. It was a stranger, but somehow, she felt familiar. Aaron had tried to look at her face, but before it came into focus his father had appeared before them, wrenching Aaron from the woman's arms and yelling at her, telling her to get away from his son.

"He's not your son!" The woman had cried. "He's mine!"

The dream had ended there, and Aaron sat bolt upright in bed.

"It was just a dream." He told himself as he struggled to control his breathing. "Just a dream." but as the dream faded, his feeling of unease remained, resilient and nagging at him until he remembered the conversation with Jesse. Throwing the covers back, he caught sight of the silvery scars that peppered his shins. Just coincidence, it must be, he probably had fallen over in a play park before and the memory of that had added authenticity to the weird dream.

"Jesse up yet?" Aaron asked as he lowered himself into his usual place at the dining table. There was no place set for his brother, which usually meant he was still sleeping. He pulled a bowl from the pile in the middle of the table and helped himself to cereal. His father was not there yet either, but judging by the bacon and eggs his mother was cooking, he would be joining them shortly.

"Jesse's eaten and gone out already." His mother replied. "I know, I was quite shocked, too." She added when she saw the incredulous look on Aaron's face.

"Shocked about what, dear?" Aaron's father asked as he appeared from the living room.

"Aaron was just asking where Jesse was."

"Oh, he's already eaten and gone out." He repeated, and Aaron nodded politely even though his mother had said the same thing just a second before.

"Any plans for today, Aaron?" His father asked, seating himself opposite at the table.

"Not really, no." Aaron smiled, pouring milk over his cereal.

"Oh good. Your mother and I have something we need to talk to you about."

51

Jesse Maysh
The day before

Uncomfortably warm from the walk home from school, Jesse let himself into the house very much looking forward to a long, cold drink. It wasn't an overly long walk, but he had been chased half way by the bully in his year – Wade Matthews – and had travelled the rest of the way at almost a jogging pace, glad that Wade had seen someone he disliked even more than Jesse and had veered off before he'd caught up to him.

"Mum, I'm home!" He called out, slinging his bag at the bottom of the stairs so that he would remember to take it up to his bedroom later on. After a moment, he realised that his mother hadn't responded, and she couldn't have gone anywhere because her car was on the drive. Maybe she was in the garden.

"Mum?"

He headed towards into the kitchen and towards the fridge, stooping to pick up a fallen piece of paper. He started to skim read it, puzzled over its wording until he spotted his mother lying unconscious on the floor nearby.

"Mum!" He yelled, leaving the letter next to the fridge and dropping down beside her. At his yell, she had stirred and he had never felt so relieved in his life.

"Jeff?" She groaned.

"No Mum, it's me, it's Jesse." He looped his arm beneath her shoulders, "Come on, let's get you off the floor." With some effort, he managed to hold onto his mum until she found her feet again and together they managed to manoeuvre her into a chair that Jesse had pulled away from the dining table with his foot.

"What happened?" He asked, as his mum leant forwards with her elbows on the table and hid her face in her hands.

"Get me some painkillers out of the cupboard would you, Jesse?" She asked, avoiding the question. Jesse nodded and retrieved them quickly. Placing them on the table in front of her, he remembered his own need for a drink and returned to the fridge to get them both one.

"I can't really remember what happened." His mum started speaking as he fixed himself a glass of juice and her a glass of water. "I was making a coffee … and then I think the doorbell rang – Oh my look at the mess!" She cried and Jesse turned his head to look. There was coffee all over the floor from where she had knocked her cup over.

"No Mum, you stay sitting down for a minute." He told her as she tried to get up, "I'll clean it."

"What did the person at the door want?" He asked as he pulled off a few too many sheets of kitchen towel and crouched down to mop up the puddle of coffee.

"Hm? Oh. I think he was delivering something a letter or..." His mother trailed off and Jesse remembered the letter he had found earlier. She was looking around the floor now, probably trying to find the letter before Jesse did.

"Is this it?" He asked, taking the coffee filled kitchen towel to the bin, wiping the excess on his trousers and grabbing the latter off the side where he'd left it. Her eyes widened for a second confirming that it was and then she tried to regain her composure.

"Oh yes, that's the one." She folded plucked it from Jesse's hand, folded it in half and placed it on the table.

"Who's it from?"

"Nobody important."

"It looked important."

"It's not."

"But it made you faint?"

"Oh, no dear, I just felt a little bit lightheaded because I haven't eaten today, that's all." Jesse looked at her with a stony expression. He knew full well she was lying because he'd had breakfast with her this morning! There was a heavy silence between them for a few seconds and Jesse finally sat down at the table taking a seat opposite his mother. He played with the glass of juice between his hands, sloshing the orange liquid back and forth. His mother watched for a few moments but didn't say anything, not even to tell him to be careful not to spill it.

"I read the letter." He announced suddenly, glancing up at her as his mother flinched.

"You. What? You read it?" Her face paled and Jesse nodded.

"What's it about Mum?" He asked, "Or who. It is about me? Or Aaron?"

"It's about your brother." She admitted finally, her voice barely more than a whisper. "We adopted him." Jesse was silent. He didn't know what to say, although his mind wouldn't shut up. This meant Aaron wasn't his real brother. Did Aaron even know? Why hadn't they ever told him. Did it mean that he was adopted, too?

"Does he know?" Jesse finally managed to ask.

"No." his mum looked away, embarrassed.

"Are you going to tell him?"

"Of course we are! How could you ask me that?" She frowned, looking offended.

"Then why doesn't he know already?"

"It... complicated. Your father and I wanted to wait until the time was right."

Jesse remembered reading something in the letter. "You mean you're only going to tell him because you have to. That's what the letter's about isn't it? Is somebody going to take him away or something?"

"No, nothing like that. Nobody is going to take Aaron away from us!" Another silence filled the room. His mother looked as though she was struggling to find the right thing to say, and Jesse was afraid of saying something he would regret. Eventually the need to ask grew too much.

"Am I adopted too?" He blurted.

"No, Jesse. You're not." He obviously didn't look very convinced, because she added; "I can show you your birth certificate if you need proof?"

"Only if you let me see Aaron's too. If his has your names on it, how does that prove I'm not adopted as well?"

His mother sighed. "Your father isn't going to like this."

"Dad's not here." He shot back, a little more forcefully than he had intended to. Rising from the table, his mother vanished into the living room. Curious about where she kept their birth certificates, he followed her and watched with wide eyes as she lifted the large, ornamental wooden cross from the wall, revealing a safe. He must have gasped, because his mother started and almost dropped the cross.

"I didn't know we had a safe."

"It's your father's, you can't let him know you've seen it." Jesse nodded in promise and moved forwards to help her lift the cross back onto the wall when she'd retrieved the documents from the safe. They took them back through to the kitchen to look at.

Jesse took the birth certificates as she handed them to him and compared them side by side. His mum had been telling the truth. Jesse's parents were listed as Jeffrey and Grace Maysh. While Aaron's mother was listed as Denise Ranlow and the father had been left blank.

A slam from the hallway made the both of them jumped and they at each other, wide eyed.

"Sorry, the wind caught the door." Jesse's father apologised as he appeared before them looking a little sheepish.

"How was work, dear?" His mother asked. Jesse wondered if she was going to tell him that she had fainted, or about the letter.

"Easy day today." His father grinned. "So I thought I'd take off early." Jesse's father worked at the local newspaper as a freelance journalist. He took mostly the community articles, and helped with the advice column from time to time.

"What's all this?" He asked, spying the papers spread out across the table.

"Ah. Yes." His mother started. "I think you should sit down first. Jesse, honey, could you go to your room and give us some privacy?"

"Hell no! I want to know what's going on."

"Watch your language, young man!" His father warned as he shrugged off his jacket and draped it over the back of a chair.

Jesse pouted, but apologised. "Can I please stay?" His mother seemed unsure, but his father nodded.

"It seems you already know some of what's going on. It is probably better you find out now than try to listen to us from the top of the stairs." Jesse looked away, but both of his parents laughed.

"We're not as dumb as you might think." His mum teased.

"So, Gracie, what's so bad that I need to sit down before knowing?" His dad asked, sliding into a chair and giving Jesse a playful shove when he rolled his eyes at the use of the name Gracie.

"The Letter came today." She said, sliding it across the table to her husband. He scooped it up and gave it a read. "It's time." She added cryptically.

It was quiet as his dad read through the letter, and Jesse felt extremely uncomfortable just sitting there watching him read. Maybe he should have gone to his room after all. The curiosity would have eaten away at him, sure. But he could have asked Aaron about it as soon as he found out. If Aaron wanted to talk to him about it. If Aaron wanted to talk to him at all afterwards.

His father put the letter down then and looked at Jesse, as if he were suddenly regretting his decision to let his youngest son remain in the kitchen with them.

"Did you read this?" He asked.

Jesse nodded. "I found it on the floor before I found Mum."

"What do you mean?" Jeff looked at his wife for an explanation, which she quickly gave.

"You know what this means, don't you?" She said sadly after reassuring him that she felt fine.

"Yes." Jesse's father replied seriously. "We can't hold it off any longer. We have to tell Aaron the truth."

Jennifer Dillon

The next morning, Doctor Roland declared Jen fit enough to go home. He gave her a few leaflets advising her to on exercising her collar bone to prevent it seizing up or setting wrong and happily escorted her to the hospital entrance. The sling they had put on her arm was itching already, and it was all she could do not to rake at it with her nails.

"Thank you." She smiled at him as her father pulled up in his car. Jen was over the moon to see that he had left the rest of the family at home for once. She waved to Doctor Roland as they pulled away and noticed John heading towards the hospital. He looked up as the car passed him, and she waved discreetly. If her father saw he would ask who it was, and then he'd probably stop the car and start an argument.

"Looking forward to being home?" Her father asked.

"Well, it's better than being in the hospital." Jen laughed. It was going to be a mad house. Elizabeth still lived with their mother, which meant that there'd also be her two sons Danny and Jake. Tamlyn also lived at home still, having been dumped by her boyfriend the moment he found out she was pregnant, so there would be pregnancy mood swings and morning sickness from her in addition to the general attitude she'd had before.

"Maybe I should come and stay with you." She looked over at her father and a queer expression crept onto his face.

"We'll see Jennybear."

Jen frowned at the use of her nickname. Her father only called her that when he wanted something or had bad news for her. She wondered if her parents had been having more arguments, they were separated but managed to get along some of the time. At the hospital they had seemed fine, but she hadn't seen them since term had started again.

Making sure her father wasn't looking, Jen reached into the sling and discreetly tried to scratch her arm. She instantly felt better.

"I wouldn't let your mother catch you doing that." Jen jumped and withdrew her hand. "She's been put on scratch patrol by that doctor of yours."

"Great."

As they pulled into the driveway, Jen's dad commented on how quiet the house was. When he'd left to pick her up, the twins had been playing Knights in the garden, whacking each other and everyone in sight with wooden swords. That had been a stupid move on someone's part. Especially when they'd realised that shins made excellent targets. Jen moved forwards to open the door but her father rushed forwards and opened it first.

"Come on Dad, I'm not an invalid."

He ignored her and went into the house. "Rachel, we're home!" He called. Jen's mother came bustling out into the front hall and enveloped Jen into her arms.

"Welcome home, darling!" She beamed.

"Where is everyone?" Jen asked.

"Oh, Elizabeth and Tamlyn have taken the twins out to the park for a little while." She replied. "Why don't you go on through to the living room, dear. I just want to have a quick word with your father."

Jen nodded and left the two of them in the hallway. From the front room she could hear her mother's hissed whispers and wondered what they could be talking about. Maybe they'd had another argument, or her father had forgotten to do something and was being called on it.

"Alright," She heard her father give in, "We'll tell her."

She ran to perch casually on the sofa when she realised they would be coming in, and was just sitting down when the front room door swung open. Her father had the look of a defeated man about him, but her mother looked triumphant, like a cat that got the best sunning spot.

"Jennifer, darling." She smiled, sitting beside her daughter on the sofa. "Your father and I need to tell you something."

Aaron Maysh

After picking his way through an agonisingly slow and silent breakfast, Aaron was tearing himself apart mentally trying to find out what it was that his parents wanted to talk to him about. Unfortunately, though, not long after breakfast had finished, he had received a call from work asking if he could do them a huge favour and cover a shift for someone who'd been in an accident on the way to work.

His father had told him to take the shift and that they could talk later – to which his mother had looked very relieved – so after a quick prayer together for the well-being of his colleague, he had left the house and gone to work. With his mind on the mysterious news all day, Aaron's shift had dragged into what felt like an eternity. When he finally clocked out, he had to resist the urge to drive home like a man possessed but still found himself turning the corner and onto his street a little earlier than he normally would have. If his father noticed – he was very particular about things like rule breaking and speeding was a big no no – Aaron could tell him that he had been let out early as thanks for working the shift, if he asked.

Walking through the front door, he was almost disappointed to smell his mother's cooking wafting tantalisingly through the air towards him. There was definitely no way his father would tell him this mysterious news before they'd eaten. Tearing up the stairs, Aaron stripped out of his work uniform and had a quick shower, barely remembering to call hello to his mother in response to her "Aaron is that you?" As he'd come through the door.

Dressing again – his father preferred them all to be at least presentable at each meal – Aaron ventured downstairs to help set the table.

"You needn't set a place for Jesse." His mother smiled over her shoulder at him when she heard him taking the plates out of the cupboard. "He's staying at James' house tonight. They have a project they need to work on for school."

Aaron frowned behind the cupboard door, it was Tuesday, and Jesse was never allowed to stay out on a school night. His stomach roiled as a million ideas about what this idea could be stampeded through his head. Hearing his father coming down the stairs from his study, Aaron finished setting the table, took his seat and waited patiently for his mother to start dishing up. She had cooked Aaron's favourite – shepherd's pie and veg. Usually he would've been over the moon, but today it filled him with dread.

His parents joined him at the table and the three of them bowed their heads, bringing their hands together in their laps.

"Our Father, who art in heaven," His father began, "hallowed be thy name. Thy Kingdom come, thy will be done, on earth as it is in heaven. Give us this day our daily bread. And forgive us our trespasses, as we forgive those who trespass against us. And lead us not into temptation, but deliver us from evil. For thine is the kingdom, the power and the glory. Forever and ever."

"Amen." The three of them spoke together. Dinner was strangely silent. Normally there would be idle chatter about what everybody had been up to during the day, but today his father scarcely looked up from his plate and his mother seemed unwilling to speak unless spoken to. She wasn't really eating either, every time Aaron looked at her, she was just pushing peas around her plate.

He would have spoken himself, but he knew the only thing to come out of his mouth would be a question and his father would only tell him to wait until after dinner when they would discuss it properly. His father had finally finished eating, seemingly unaware that Aaron and

Grace had been watching his final mouthfuls and suggested that they all go into the living room. And that they could clear the dishes afterwards.

The three of them moved into the living room, with his parents sitting side by side on the sofa and Aaron sitting opposite them in the armchair. He picked at a hole that was starting to form in the knee of his jeans, feeling almost like he was in a job interview or an interrogation.

"Aaron. As we mentioned this morning, there is something that your mother and I would like to talk to you about." Aaron only nodded in response, feeling the knot inside him constrict painfully in anticipation and fearing that his voice would fail him if he spoke.

"I think it would be easiest if first of all we show you the letter." His father started to rise from the sofa but his mother was shaking her head.

"I do not see why we have to." She whispered.

"You know why, Gracie."

"But everything's going to change."

Aaron blanched for a moment, and wondered if maybe his mother was unwell. She certainly looked a little off, and her behaviour all day had been weird. Was it serious? Was she going to die? After some encouragement from his father, his mother opened a draw in the coffee table and pulled out a letter, reluctantly passing it across to Aaron. The header seemed to be from a hospital or something. His eyes widened as the word Cancer flashed across his mind. Forcing himself to concentrate, he blinked away the horrid thought and read the letter properly.

HUNTER & SAMPSON SCIENCE ENTERPRISES

Dear Mr. and Mrs. Maysh.

It is with great pleasure that we write to you on this special occasion. 19 years ago today, you, we and science embarked on a great journey of discovery that is set to change the future of mankind. The children have now come of age, and it is time for Project P.C. to really begin. Of the 10, you were entrusted with the life and care of #01 under the conditions that you raise the child, and under no circumstances, let them find out about the experiment until authorised to do so.

I, Dr. Jeremy Hunter hereby authorise you to explain everything to #01 so that the next phase of the experiment can begin. We have set up a page on the HSSE website to provide additional information as we are sure that there will be many questions during this transitional period. However, this site will require a special log in. This, the password, and the website address itself can be found on the reverse of this letter.

Yours sincerely,

Dr. J. A. Hunter

Aaron looked at the letter incredulously. Ok, so it wasn't cancer but he wasn't quite sure what it meant, or why it had been sent to them in the first place. Who or what was #01 and why were his parents meant to be raising it?

"What is this?" Aaron asked finally, holding it back out to his mother to save himself from reading it over and over. "What on earth is Project P.C. and who or what is number one?" There were so many questions racing though his mind and fighting to be asked.

"There's no easy way to say this, so I'm just going to come out and say it … Aaron, your Mother and I … Well, we're not your biological parents." Aaron felt like his whole world was being pulled out from underneath him.

"What do you mean you're not my real parents?" The letter couldn't be about him. It couldn't. It wasn't.

His mother finally found her voice. "We adopted you, Aaron. 19 years ago. We're not your biological parents but are still your real parents." she told him, "Your father and I had been trying to conceive for years, and then this opportunity came up, and we decided to take it as a sign."

"I'm adopted." He repeated, as if hearing the words come out of his own mouth would make it a concrete fact. "I am … what about Jesse?"

"Oh, honey, no, honey. Jesse's ours."

"So I am not yours?" His hands curled into fists at his sides. Part of his mind was telling himself to calm down, but another, louder, part was telling him that he had every right to be angry. His parents – who weren't actually his parents – had lied to him for his whole life. Had allowed him to think himself part of their family.

"Of course you are! That's not what I meant at all." His mother blurted.

"So what's this about?" He demanded, pointing an angry finger at the letter his mother held. It was a good job he had given it back to her, or he might have shredded it by now. He was still tempted to, as if destroying the letter could destroy this news.

"Aaron, please calm down." His father spoke. He was using his calm voice, the one he used to settle family disputes. It usually worked, but right now Aaron resented it. That surprised him. He'd never really been an angry person.

"What is it?" He asked again, managing to make his voice sound calm and very glad that his mother and father couldn't see the mess he was on the inside. His father was the one who spoke now, no doubt because of the frantic he had received from his wife.

"You know how adoption works, right, Aaron?" Aaron nodded. "Well, your mother and I didn't use conventional methods to adopt you." his father paused, as if trying to think up the right way to say whatever it was he wanted to say. "We saw an advert in a scientific journal." Aaron must have pulled a face because his father paused and added. "I know what you are thinking. Why was I reading one? Well, I had just started working at the newspaper and I was doing some research for a story I was working on. In the back of the journal there was an advert explaining that some scientists were looking for people to adopt some newborns. Your mother and I had been trying to conceive

65

for almost three years, so when we found this advert we decided to take it as a sign from God. That he wanted us to try and save a child from a life of science. So we looked into it – and in the end, they gave us you."

"Why were scientists giving away babies for adoption?"

"They're running an experiment to try and solve what they believe to be an overpopulation crisis in the making."

"So I'm an experiment?" Aaron asked, suddenly worried. What the hell had been done to him? Had he been born in a laboratory and tested on? "The numbers on the letter – I'm not the only one, am I?"

"No." His father sighed. "We would have saved them all if we could, but they wanted them to go to different homes. There are ten of you in total."

"Did they do anything to us? In the laboratory?"

"I'd rather not tell you."

"Why not?"

"Why not?" Aaron repeated after his father said nothing. He tried to retain the calmness in his voice, and managed it, just barely.

"You really want to know?" His father sighed and rubbed the bridge of his nose as Aaron nodded. "We were hoping that we could just forget about all this. Your mother and I were only contracted to tell you about the experiment at a certain point in your life, not to enforce anything afterwards. Just forget it all now, Aaron. Before you learn more than you'd like to. Just turn away from it all and let us go back to how we were."

"Wait, so if this letter had never arrived you just never would have told me?" Aaron asked.

"Well, yes. What point would there have been in filling your head full of these doubts? You are our son, Aaron, whether you our blood flows through your veins or not. We raised you. We are your family."

"I also thought that this family was above lying to each other! That we believed in honesty and openness. What else have you lied to me about?" Aaron found himself on his feet now, and he had taken a step towards his father.

"Do not raise your voice at me!" His father growled, taking a step forwards and closing the gap between the two of them. For a moment, Aaron wondered if he was going to reach out and throttle him or something.

"We haven't lied to you about anything!" His mother answered. Aaron turned and found her standing next to him with a hand placed cautiously on his arm. "Come and sit down, Aaron."

He tugged his arm out of her grasp. "I need to get out of here – I need to think." he turned on his heel and sped towards the front door. Pulling his coat from It is hook, he dragged it out of the door behind him, slamming it shut as his mother yelled, "What time will you be home?" Home. Ha.

Aaron's head felt full, stuffed to the brim with thoughts. They were all fighting for position, jostling about in his mind, all wanting to be thought about at once. Taking a left on the next street over, Aaron decided to go to the only place he knew that would help him to sort out his head.

Jennifer Dillon

"I can't believe this is happening." Jen moaned, grabbing one of Sam's pillows and pulling it over her face. Sam – or Samantha as she was known by her parents – was Jen's best friend. They met in secondary school and managed to keep it going even though they were now in universities at opposite ends of the country. Thank god for video calling.

A couple of hours after enduring the conversation with her parents, Jen had made her excuses and escaped to Sam's house. Thankfully she had been home and Jen hadn't been forced to go back home.

"Oh dear, what have they done now?" Sam asked, trying to pry the pillow away from Jen's face. "Come on, give it to me. I can't understand a word you say when you are under there."

Jen pouted under the pillow, before swinging it away and bopping Sam on the head with it. She laughed as Sam's face morphed from concern into shock, and her lips formed an "O".

"You did not just hit me with that!" She exclaimed. Jen bopped her again.

"Count yourself lucky you have that." Sam glared, pointing at the splint "But I'll get you back, you'll see."

Jen shrugged, "Whatever you say, Sammy." She hit her with the pillow again.

"That's it! Injured or not, I'm going to tickle you to death." Sam whooped and pounced on her friend, poking around her ribs and under her arms while Jen tried to fend her off one-armed and with just a pillow for protection. Ten minutes later, with their ribs and lungs aching

68

from laughing so much, the two of them sat on the floor at the end of Sam's bed.

"So, are you going to tell me now?" Sam asked, wiggling her fingers menacingly.

"Okay," Jen sighed, pulling her pillow to her stomach and wrapping her arms around it carefully. She took a deep breath and looked Sam in the eyes.

"My parents are getting back together."

Sam's eyes widened and amazingly, she managed not to laugh. "that is your big dilemma?"

Jen glared at her. "It's huge! They're absolutely terrible for each other. Every time they get back together they break up again!"

"Jen, they're adults. They're quite capable of making their own decisions."

"But what if It is the wrong one? What if they just end up hurting each other again?"

"It is not your problem. You don't have to worry about it. If this doesn't work out again, then it'll be nobody's fault but their own, okay?" Sam turned to Jen to make sure she was looking at her. "It will not be your fault. It wasn't your fault the first time around, either!" She added when Jen opened her mouth to protest.

"I know it's not my fault." She admitted, "But sometimes it feels like it is. Like I somehow managed to drive a wedge between them and they just couldn't get around it."

Sam moved forwards and carefully enveloped Jen in her arms.

"Look you dummy, it is not your fault and it never was. I'm sure if you go home and ask your parents about it, they'll tell you exactly what I told you. You'll see."

"You're right. Maybe I should go home and apologise for running off earlier."

Sam nodded. "You know you're welcome here if you need to hide out." She grinned.

"Yeah, sorry about just turning up."

"Don't worry about it, you know my mum would've let you in and fed you if I hadn't been here." Sam told her. "Gimme a ring later so I can say I told you so, okay?" Sam smiled as she led Jen to the door.

Jen laughed and punched her playfully on the arm. "Sure. See you later." Stood outside Sam's front door, Jen wasn't sure she was ready to go home yet. The new lovey dovey parents waiting for her were always such a culture shock compared to her old bitter parents even though she knew it wouldn't last.

Even walking slow, it only took Jen fifteen minutes to reach her house and she was surprised at how different the atmosphere in the house was as she opened the door. From the living room, she could hear her parents yelling. Wow – that had to be a new personal best even for them. How long had she been gone? An hour? Two tops.

"I am saying no!" She heard her father yell.

"We don't have a choice, we signed a contract!"

"I don't care! I am forbidding you to say anything about it!"

"You forbid me?" Her mother's voice was getting sharper, "You do not own me, you can't tell me what to do."

"We agreed! You agreed that we would never mention it. That we would just pretend it never happened!" After a breeze made Jen shiver, she realised that she hadn't shut the front door. Stepping inside the house, she let the door slam shut. The house instantly fell silent.

"Jen, is that you?" Her mother called. Who else would it be?

"Yeah Mum, it's me." She called back. She thought she could hear the hissing of whispers, as if her parents were carrying on their argument but didn't want her to hear. It was a bit late for them to start trying to shield her from their arguments now. Her childhood had been full of them.

She'd always felt like she was the cause of it all, even though her parents had never specifically mentioned that she was, and she couldn't explain why she thought it.

"Is something wrong?" She asked her parents as they came out of the living room and into the hallway.

"Of course not dear. Just a disagreement is all." Her mother smiled. Jen frowned, she'd learnt to recognise that smile too. It was meant to reassure her that everything was fine, but it never quite reached her mother's eyes. Most of the time it just made her feel worse.

Graham Ahern

"Graham, Dr. Wainright is ready to see you now." A pleasant female voice called from the desk just beyond the door to the waiting room. Throwing the magazine he'd been lazily leafing through to one side, Graham rose to his feet and exited the waiting room. He hated being in there. The decorators had obviously tried to make it look cosy, but they had missed the mark by a long shot and it looked clinical. Well, at least it didn't smell like a hospital.

"Thanks, Penny." Graham grinned at the girl behind the reception desk. She looked up from her magazine and smiled at him. At least if he sat in the right place in the waiting room, he could peek out at Penny whenever she was looking the opposite direction. He continued through the reception area to an opaque glass door that read:

Dr. Samantha Wainright
Psychiatrist.

Graham opened the door to Dr. Wainright's office and found her in her usual position behind the glass desk that occupied the corner of the room in front of the window. She looked up from her notes and smiled but didn't rise until Graham had come all the way into the room and shut the door behind himself. Every time he saw that stupid glass desk he wondered how it was never covered in fingerprints.

"Good morning, Graham. How are you doing this morning?" She asked him. Her voice was calm and soothing. Probably something you had to practice when becoming a psychiatrist.

"'M doin' good." Graham mumbled. It was a complete lie, and he knew that she would see through him anyway.

"Okay. How about we take a seat and get started then?" She turned and walked over to the chair she used for their sessions - a comfy looking, green arm chair and sank into it, pulling her clipboard and pen from the table where she kept them ready and waiting.

Graham shuffled after her and took his seat opposite her on a matching green sofa that looked a lot comfier than it was. The kind that looked like you'd sink into it when really it was solid. He supposed it was to prevent people from falling asleep during their sessions. Leaning forwards slightly, he pulled his arms free of his jacket and threw it over the arm rest at the other end of the sofa.

"So, Graham, how have things been at home this week?" Dr. Wainright asked.

Graham thought about lying, but he knew that she would just draw it out of him eventually.

"They've been arguing again." He started, meaning his parents. "This time about a letter they got."

Dr. Wainright nodded as she took notes. "Do you know what the letter was about?"

"Yeah." Graham paused, and fidgeted with his sleeve. "Dad said I am not s'posed to tell anyone about it. He said He'd batter me if I did."

"You can tell me, Graham." Dr. Wainright smiled, "Your father doesn't know about our sessions does he?" Graham shook his head. Neither of his parents knew he was seeing a psychiatrist and he wanted it to stay that way. At first it had been court ordered after he had been caught bullying other children at his school, but now he was going because he didn't want to give up hope. Even if he still bullied, he liked to believe that one day he could change himself, he just had to get strong enough first.

His aunt – the only nice one – had fronted the cost of his sessions. Graham also knew that she had tried to fight for custody of him once, which was why his mum didn't speak to her any more.

"The letter was about me."

"And was it a good letter, or a bad letter?"

"I dunno. Bit of both?"

"And how did that make you feel?"

"Confused." Graham shifted on the sofa a little and dug his hand into his pocket. "I managed to get a copy of the letter so you could read it."

"Well done, Graham." Dr. Wainright leant forwards and plucked the folded letter from Graham's fingers. He waited patiently while she read through it, wondering what she was going to make of it, or whether she would have already known. She managed to keep her face completely professional – almost expressionless giving nothing away.

"So, what is good about this letter?" Dr. Wainright asked when she finally looked up again.

"Well, it means I'm adopted. I am not related to them!" Graham grinned, "So maybe I won't be like them."

"That is true."

"And it means that there are other people like me out there. I don't have to be alone any more. Maybe I can make some friends."

Dr. Wainright wrote all of this down. "And what are the bad things about it?"

"Well dad says there's no escaping fate." Graham frowned, "And it don't matter that I ain't blood, 'cause they raised me as their own."

"Is there anything else that is either good or bad about the letter?"

"Yeah. Mum and dad had an argument 'cause she let me read it and he didn't want me to. But then he said that now I knew, and the contract they had signed was up – so he could finally leave. He said that the only reason he had stayed around to raise me was 'cause of the contract they signed, and the money they were getting paid to do it."

Graham had brought his legs up now, resting the heels of his feet against the edge of the sofa and wrapping his arms around his knees.

"And what happened after that?" Dr. Wainright asked from her chair. She never moved during their sessions, and Graham was glad for it. If she moved towards him – touched him even – he'd probably break down and allow himself to cry in front of someone. He never allowed that to happen, not even at home when one of his parents decided to beat him in a drunken rage. Since the age of seven, he had been taught by his father to be a strong and proud boy, and not to cry like a cowardly girl.

"Dad stormed out, and mum went straight to the fridge."

"She started drinking?"

Graham snorted. "She'd already been drinking. She just started drinking more."

"Have you thought about leaving?" Dr. Wainright asked him sincerely.

"I dunno where I'd would go."

"What about your aunt?"

"I hadn't thought about it." Well, that wasn't true. He'd thought about it once before, but when he'd mentioned it, his parents had threatened him and his dad had lobbed a beer bottle at him. He had been too scared to bring it up again. And he was reluctant to take the fight to his aunt's house, not when she was already defying his parents by paying for these sessions.

Dr. Wainright smiled, "I think that perhaps you should." Then she looked up at the clock. "I think we should leave our session here for today, Graham." Carefully placing her clipboard and pen on the table beside the chair, she finally rose from her seat.

Graham mirrored her movement, plucking his jacket from the arm of the sofa and pulling it on. "Thank you Dr. Wainright." Graham

75

managed a small smile as he exited her office. "Bye Penny." He called to the secretary as he passed her desk. Pulling his jacket tighter, Graham stepped out of the building and started his long walk home. Before he had taken even ten steps, a shrill cry stopped him in his tracks.

"What the hell were you doing in there?"

Graham blanched as he turned and saw his mother stomping towards him. Knowing that he would regret it later, Graham did the first thing that came to mind.

He ran.

Farrell Brennan

Farrell said his goodbyes to Davy at the door. Their activities the night before had gone a bit further than Farrell had planned and he was still as confused about his feelings as ever. It wasn't that he had enjoyed what they had done, exactly the opposite. It was all just going a bit too fast; the alcohol was probably to blame there, and his body hadn't reacted in the way he'd wanted it to, which had been a bit embarrassing though Davy had been really great about it. In any case, Farrell just wanted to be alone for a while to think things over.

Not bothering to look where he was going, he bumped into someone and the two of them fell to the ground. As he sat up and started to apologise, he realised who it was that he had bumped into and scooted back away from him. He didn't know the boy's name, but he was a bully. Every time he saw Farrell, he would attack him either physically or verbally.

"I'm sorry – I didn't mean to." Farrell blurted, even though he wasn't completely to blame.

"Get lost, fag." The boy grunted, looking around to make sure no-one else had seen what had happened. "Get the hell out of here before I kick your fucking ass." Farrell didn't need telling twice and he had no idea why he had been let go, but who was he to argue with fate.

At least today he wouldn't be going home with a black eye that his family would assume was because he was trying to cope with his whole adoption issue. Hearing footsteps behind him, Farrell quickened his pace worried that his tormentor had changed his mind and was coming to fulfil his promise. Relief flooded through him when he heard someone yell for him to slow down. Slowing down a little he turned and found his best friend, Troy, jogging to catch up with him.

"What are you doing out here?" Farrell asked.

"I might ask you the same question." His friend retorted.

"I just wanted some alone time is all. Don't think I haven't noticed you all babysitting me since that letter came."

Troy pretended to be hurt. "As if I would do such a thing!" Farrell raised an eyebrow at him. "Well okay, maybe I would. But I was just trying to make sure you are really okay."

"Do I look okay?"

"Well yeah I guess so."

"So you can stop trying to make sure then!"

"But that is what's so worrying!"

"That makes no sense."

Troy sighed. "I guess I just don't understand why you haven't freaked the hell out. I know I would have!"

Farrell shrugged. "Being adopted isn't that big a deal. Just because my mum didn't give birth to me doesn't mean she's not my mum any more. Nothing has changed, in my eyes anyway, it's everyone else that's making such a big deal out of it."

It was Troy's turn to raise an eyebrow, as if he didn't really believe what Farrell was saying and after a moment he sighed. "Well, okay dude. If you say you are okay then I'll believe you."

"Thanks Troy." Farrell grinned, before being rewarded with a pat on the back.

"What are friends for?" Troy laughed, "So what are you getting me for my birthday?"

Farrell laughed and punched his friend on the arm. "I don't know yet. Maybe a clue?"

Maybe Troy would stop treating him so differently now. He'd been starting to think he'd become some sort of a leper. His parents being weird about it was expected, but Troy had been the one person he'd hoped would treat it like it was no big deal. Just another day in their lives. It had hurt that even his best friend had started walking on eggshells around him.

Flashback
Grace Maysh

"Grace, you're making a mess." Jeff murmured to her. She looked down at her lap and realised that she'd been pulling a tissue to pieces and covering herself in it.

"Whoops." She carefully started to brush it all into a pile before tipping it into an empty sandwich bag she found in the glove compartment of their car. Staring out of the window, she fell deep into thought once again. Today they were going to the laboratory to pick up their baby.

She and Jeff had tried to conceive naturally and would never have considered adoption if they were able to do so. They'd found out about this opportunity purely by chance after her husband had come across an advert.

"It's a sign!" Jeff had exclaimed, "I think God wants us to save this poor little soul." The baby was part of an experiment to prevent an overpopulation crisis from occurring in the next hundred years or so.

"God would never let that happen." Jeff had said. Apparently, the child had been given an implant to control his hormones, at first Grace had been worried that this was going to be hugely noticeable – they were supposed to be keeping this a secret – but Dr. Hunter had assured them that the implant was well hidden. Even the scar from the insertion would be hidden in their hairline when the child got older. She still worried though. What if Dr. Hunter had lied and the child was deformed or something. Would she be able to see past the implant and love this child? Would she be able to raise him as her own?

She had no choice now of course; the contract had been signed and they had chosen his name; Aaron. Mostly because it had been Jeff's father's name. But also partially because he was the first child of ten and the scientists had decided that the children should be named alphabetically according to their ID number. Probably to make them seem more like experiments and less like actual children.

The other parents would be collecting their children today, too. Though the scientists had informed them that meeting them was entirely optional. At first Grace had been unsure. Maybe she would rather not know, that way she could pass them in the street and not wonder whether they were thinking all the terrible things she'd been thinking or find out that the other parents were managing fine if she struggled. In the end, Jeff had talked her round, explaining that it would help to know that they aren't alone in this. And maybe they could help each other.

"Like a support group." He had suggested, "They'll be the only other people going through what we're going through. I'm sure they're all just as worried as we are."

Dragging her gaze away from the window Grace looked over at her husband. He was always there for her – her pillar of strength. There was no way she was going to have to do this alone.

"What?" He smiled as he realised she was watching him.

"Do I need a reason to look at you?"

"Well, no."

"Good." She grinned. "What is it?" She added as his expression changed.

"We're here."

Grace turned her attention forwards and saw a modest sign pointing into a long, gravelled driveway. The building it led up to was very old and beautiful. The walls were red brick, and each of the many windows was trimmed with white – matching the front door – it was hard to believe that this building was home to a laboratory and not a museum.

"Oh look, we're not the first ones here." She noticed some other cars parked outside the house. Jeff pulled up beside the end car and they got out, in awe of the building. It was a lot more beautiful close up.

"Shall we?" Jeff smiled, holding out his arm. They were greeted just inside the door by a tall, lean woman with long, brown hair. She wore a severe skirt suit and heels.

"Good morning!" She beamed, sounding a lot friendlier than she looked. "My name is Vivienne, I'm Dr. Hunter's personal secretary." Jeff and Grace nodded politely.

"You must be Mr. and Mrs. Maysh." She checked their names quickly on a clipboard in one hand in front of her. "Everybody else has already arrived. Dr. Hunter just has something he wants to ask you before we introduce you to your child. If you'd like to follow me, I'll take you to his office now." She led them down a corridor and to an elevator. As she selected a floor, Grace wondered exactly how many floors there were beneath the building. From the outside it had looked as though there were only three or four floors, but the elevator panel listed a lot more. She couldn't tell exactly how many however, because Vivienne was blocking it but definitely more than four.

When they exited, they were led down a hallway to a door with a small silver name plate.

Dr. J. A. Hunter
Lead Research Scientist
Hunter and Sampson Science Enterprises

After only a single brusque knock, they were led into the room.

"Ah! Good morning!" The man in the room grinned, putting his coffee down and rising from his seat. "Jeff, Grace. It's so good to see you again. How are we feeling? Excited? Terrified? Both?"

"Definitely both." Jeff answered, shaking the doctor's hand. Grace was more than happy to let her husband do the talking for now.

"Excellent!" He continued. "I wanted to ask you something. The other parents are here and have already agreed to this, but I don't want that force your decision at all." He paused for a second before continuing. "I know that we originally planned for everyone to meet up afterwards, but would it be possible for you to all meet up now, that way I can do the tour as a group, and just section you off into different rooms afterwards to meet your new child."

"Of course, that's fine." Jeff smiled, curling an arm around his wife to make her feel better. She looked up at him imploringly, and he just smiled at her, leaning in a little to kiss her on the forehead making her feel better.

"Brilliant." Dr. Hunter smiled. "If you'd like to come with me, then."

Grace suppressed a whimper as they entered a room and eighteen sets of eyes looked up at them. She hated being put in the centre of attention, it normally ended in her getting embarrassed and falling over or something. She didn't have to worry for long though, because Dr. Hunter swept into the room and clapped his hands, taking all of the attention with him.

"Now then, welcome all of you, to the Hunter and Sampson Science Enterprises Laboratory. We are about to give you a short-ish tour of our laboratories, and then it will be time for you to meet your new children." An excited murmur floated through the room and reminded Grace of school field trips when everyone would whisper amongst themselves about the things they wanted to see the most, or what they wanted to do next.

Holding onto Jeff's hand tightly, they followed after the group as Dr. Hunter led them around. All of the science apparatus and machinery was very daunting to her, and she had no idea how her husband was finding it. She knew very well that he wasn't a fan of science. He always said that being a man of religion took precedence, and that science was playing god. No matter how many diseases had been cured or prevented because of it.

The tour had been as short as promised, and she wondered whether there were places that they weren't allowed to go, or that the scientists didn't want them to see. As the laboratory door whooshed shut behind them, they found themselves in a round room with doors leading off it.

"This is the ante chamber." Dr. Hunter explained to them. "As you can see, there are 10 doors and each of them are numbered. The number on the door corresponds with the number of your child, so please make your way to your assigned rooms, and your children will be brought in to you momentarily."

Everyone seemed curious to see who had been given which number, and they all found themselves pausing at the door to have a sheepish look around. Realising that they'd all done exactly the same thing, they laughed entered their rooms in unison.

Grace was relieved when Jeff reached out and turned the handle. An irrational thought had flown through her mind that if she touched it, it might not let her in. As he opened the door, she wondered whether their baby would be hooked up to any weird machines and shuddered, trying to get the idea out of her mind.

Thankfully, the room was empty except for a padded table in the centre and some armchairs. Grace breathed a sigh of relief and went to the closest armchair, placing her handbag on the cushion. There was a second door on the opposite side of the room, so they each sat in a chair that faced it, Grace perching beside her handbag. For what seemed like an age, they waited for that second door to open. Finally, the door handle moved and Grace found herself reliving all the morbid thoughts she had gone through earlier. Now was the moment of truth.

A female nurse entered the room carrying their baby boy. Grace found herself releasing a breath she hadn't realised she'd been holding.

"He's beautiful!" She cried, rising from her seat and rushing over to the woman. She managed to catch herself before snatching the baby from the woman's arms though, and held out her hands.

"He's all yours." The nurse chuckled at Grace's eagerness and held the baby out to her.

Grace's eyes widened and for a moment she didn't dare touch him in case she dropped him. Something touched her and she flinched, looking around to see Jeff placing a reassuring hand on her shoulder. He nodded in encouragement and she reached out to take the child. Their child. He was gorgeous, with a fine coating of black hair across his scalp and wonderful, expressive, forest green eyes. As she admired him, all of her thoughts and worries vanished.

"Have you decided on a name yet?" The nurse asked, having taken a small step backwards to let the new parents start bonding with their son.

Grace nodded. "His name is Aaron."

"That's a beautiful name. I'll be right back." The nurse vanished back through the door, leaving Grace and Jeff alone with the baby.

"Would you like to hold him?" Grace asked, smiling up at her husband. He nodded and easily scooped the baby out of her arms. A natural already. As she passed him over, Grace spied the scar on the back of Aaron's head. It was nowhere near as bad as she'd imagined that it would be, and true to Dr. Hunter's word it would be hidden more as his hair grew.

The nurse reappeared, bringing with her a trolley laden with a large blue shoulder bag and some parcels.

"All of these are for you." She laughed when their expressions changed. "A gift, and also a starter pack. Everything you need for the first week of Aaron's life with you – except of course for the furniture. But I'm sure you've already sorted that out."

Grace grinned sheepishly. They'd sorted the nursery the very same day they'd received their confirmation letter.

"It's a good job we came in the car." Jeff laughed.

Present day
Aaron Maysh

Aaron's knees ached. Ever since escaping his house earlier, he had been in the local church – St. Mary's. Praying did a lot to help clear the mind, but it was hell on the knees; even when you used one of the prayer cushions.

A rustling noise behind him announced the presence of someone else, and he turned to look. Reverend Jacobs was towering over him with a concerned look on his face.

"That is a mighty long prayer."

Aaron chuckled. "Yeah, God's probably stopped listening by now."

"He's always listening. But if you had like an extra set of ears just in case, feel free to talk to me." Reverend Jacobs sat down and patted the space beside him on the pew.

Reluctantly, Aaron rose from the prayer cushion, picking it up and popping it back on its hook. He was quite tempted to just leave, but that meant going home already and he wasn't ready for that just yet. He took the seat beside the priest anyway but didn't say anything. The Reverend seemed happy enough to just sit there waiting for Aaron to open up to him.

"I'm not sure you'd understand."

"I think you might be surprised, I've heard a great many things in my time. And it is not my place to Judge. Only to listen."

"I just found out I'm adopted." Aaron admitted after another long pause.

"Ah. I was expecting this to happen eventually."

"Wait – you knew?"

Reverend Jacobs nodded pensively. "I remember your father visiting me before you came to live with them."

"Oh." Aaron should have expected that, really. "What did he say? Or is there some kind of Reverend – confessor confidentiality clause?"

"Oh, I am sure that neither God or your father would mind if I told you." Rev. Jacobs fell silent, and Aaron wondered whether he was going to tell him, or whether he was just trying to remember – it had been almost twenty years ago.

As Aaron opened his mouth to ask, The Reverend continued. "Your father seemed just as troubled then as you do now. He was confused about the message God was trying to send him. You see, your father grew up in a society where the sciences were heavily disapproved of. They taught that science was trying to disprove God's existence and go against his will."

Aaron nodded, he knew his father's stance on science. You should never mention the creation versus evolution argument unless you wanted to experience it first hand for days.

"He was very troubled in the days and weeks leading up to your adoption. He didn't know whether involving himself in the world of science would be a good or a bad thing. I counselled him."

"So you told him to adopt me?"

"No. I just helped him to realise the decision he had already made in his heart."

"I just can't see why they didn't tell me. All these years and they pretended that I was their own flesh and blood. Not of some stranger who didn't want me."

"It is partially do with with a contract of secrecy that your parents were forced to sign by the scientists, but I also think that in keeping it from you, your father thought he could give you more of a normal life. He did what he thought was best for you and the family. I know it hasn't been easy for him to lie to you. He thinks about it every day. I'm sure your mother does too, although she doesn't visit the church quite so often as your father does."

"He comes here a lot?" Aaron asked. As far as he knew, his parents only came to church for the Sunday services, or any other special announcements that might be happening during the month.

"Increasingly so in the last couple of months. He's been worried about telling you, fearing that you might turn away from them." The two of them paused when they heard the heavy church doors open. They were sat behind a pillar, and not visible to whoever had just come in.

"Aaron, are you here?" It was his father. Aaron's eyes widened and he sank in his seat a little.

"If you don't wish to go with him now, it's your choice." The vicar whispered to him before rising from his seat beside Aaron and going to welcome his father.

"Ah, Jeff. To what do we owe this pleasure this evening?"

"Reverend Jacobs, have you seen Aaron at all?"

"I have indeed."

"Is he still here?"

"I'm here." Aaron announced, standing up and peeking around the pillar. A look of relief flooded his father's face, and guilt flooded through him.

"I'm sorry I ran away like that." He mumbled as he joined his father and the vicar.

"And I'm sorry that we couldn't tell you sooner but this doesn't change anything Aaron, you are still our son for as long as you want to be." Aaron rushed forwards and wrapped his arms around his father, something he hadn't done in years. He felt his father soften and they hugged in silence for a moment.

"Shall we go home then?" Aaron asked, raising a smile from his father.

"Yes, I think your mother will be worried enough without me vanishing as well."

Aaron laughed, "Yeah, she might be fully grey by the time we get back." He turned, wanting to thank the vicar for his help, but he had already left the two of them to it, vanishing silently into the back of the church. Wondering how he had managed to miss the priest leaving, Aaron left the church with his father, giving a quick thank you to God as they closed the heavy doors and headed for the car.

Dr. Jeremy Hunter

Having been working steadily and uninterrupted for the past couple of hours, Jeremy gave a small jolt of surprise when his computer beeped at him. He hastily finished his sentence, musing over the fact that he would probably have trouble reading his handwriting again later on. Maybe he'd get Vivienne to type it up, she could understand his appalling writing.

The beep had been an email notification, and when he opened it he found that it wasn't in his normal email account, but in the one he'd had set up specifically for Project. P.C. For the parents, in case they needed to contact him. His father hadn't thought it was necessary to do so, preferring to contact them by phone or letter. But Jeremy preferred it this way. The use of the internet and emails had been growing at the time. "We have to keep up with communication technology." He had told his father.

In the end the account had been used only a handful of times, and he was almost glad that his father wasn't around to rub it in his face. This email was the first one the account had received in almost five years. It was from a D. Harper. The name sounded vaguely familiar and he chewed on the end of his pen and thought about it. Ah yes, one of the parents was David Harper. Father of Number Four, he believed. Curious, he opened the email.

Dear Dr. Hunter,
My name is Dominic Harper. (Although perhaps you know me better as #04?) I would like

to get to know the other members of this experiment, and I was wondering if you would be able to provide me with any contact details?

I asked my parents, but they told me that they don't have any information about the others so I was hoping you'd be able to help me.

Yours Sincerely,
Dominic Harper.

Ahh, so it was David's son! He'd forgotten that they shared their initials. Bemused, Jeremy re-read the email a couple of times before hitting reply. He had been expecting questions about the others in the experiment, but nowhere near this soon. He wondered whether Dominic's parents knew that he had contacted them before realising that they must have given him the email address. There was one listed on the site the ten had been given in the letter they received but that was a different account.

Dear Dominic,

Unfortunately, I cannot disclose to you the information requested as it would go against the data protection act, as well as my scientific curiosity.

I wish to observe how each subject will seek out and connect with the others, and handing out their information would prove unfair to those who may not want to be contacted.

Sincerely,
Dr. J. A. Hunter.

Dominic Harper

Dominic sighed and closed his emails. He'd been so sure that Dr. Hunter would say yes, and he would finally be a step closer to contacting the others. Although what he would have actually said to them once he got their email addresses or phone numbers was a whole different ballgame entirely. Phone calls gave him anxiety, he supposed it was a form of phobia, but he hated to use the phone. Whenever it would ring he would stare at it, hesitating. Should he answer, or just ignore it? If it was an unknown number, he would mostly just ignore it and hope that they left a voice mail if it was important.

Emails though, were comfortable. He could say exactly what he wanted to say without sounding like an idiot or stammering because of nerves. You could spend time writing an email, getting it to look and sound exactly how you wanted it, not like in a conversation over the phone.

Disappointed in the response he had received; he pushed the thoughts away and decided to amuse himself on the internet for a little while. There were a couple of sites that he liked to frequent, places where he could talk to people, and make friends. Forums, they were called. He paused, eyes opening wide in realisation. That's it! What if he made his own forum, just a simple one where he could try and get to know the others in the experiment with him – and maybe he could email Dr. Hunter again and ask if he'd be willing to help. If he said no, he could always try and hack the site to place a link there himself. Not that he was any good at hacking, but y'know, last resort kind of thing.

He found a website that offered free forum hosting easy enough, but what should he call it? He decided to look through the Hunter and Sampson Science Enterprises site and see whether there was anything in there that would make a good name. As he waited for the site to load, the song on his computer changed and he hummed along to the song for a while, before realising he could use some of the lyrics. Soul Echo. It was perfect. It sounded interesting, and he thought it would be a kind of play on words with the whole compatible partner thing.

It didn't take long to make the forum – he actually spent longer trying to think up a user name he could go by. In the end he chose D0M1N1C. Yes, that would do. Now to try Dr. Hunter again. Quickly opening his emails again he penned a quick message.

Dear Dr. Hunter.
OK. I understand. Instead, would it be possible for you to add a link to the front page of your website? I've created a forum to try and work towards getting to know the other nine, and for all of us to get to know each other on an 'even playing field' as it were. This way, the other nine can choose to ignore the link if they don't wish to get in contact with myself or any of the others. The website URL is:
http://www.SoulEcho.com
Sincerely,
Dominic Hunter.

Sitting back in his chair and re-reading the email a couple times, Dominic decided he was happy with what he had written and clicked send. Hopefully, Dr. Hunter would be more willing to this idea. Dom was looking forward to getting to know the other nine and he often wondered how they had reacted to the news, probably not with the same understanding and intrigue that he had. Once when he was younger – in his early teens if he remembered correctly - Dominic had fallen off a swing set and cracked his head open. At the hospital, they'd taken some head scans to make sure there were no brain injuries and when the doctor had come to show his parents the results, he'd seen something weird. It looked kind of like there was a microchip or something in his head. His parents had very quickly told him that there was nothing there and ushered him out of the room to wait while they continued speaking to the doctor.

When he had later tried to ask the doctor, he had fobbed him off and told him that it was just a malfunction on the scanner. Back then, Dominic had been in his 'aliens are out there' phase for weeks he'd been sure that he'd been abducted and that his every move was now being monitored by some kind of intergalactic being.

Now, he knew different. Clerical error indeed. There had been something in his head, and he knew now what it was. He'd been microchipped, something they had had done to their new dog only last week. Absent mindedly rubbing the back of his head where he could feel the small rise of a scar in his hair, he wondered if the procedure had been at all similar.

Dr. Jeremy Hunter

Jeremy had given up checking his emails for now. He had hoped that Dominic might reply, and ask further questions, but after an hour and still nothing he had resigned himself back to his work. Deciding that he'd had enough of sitting at his desk, he rose, hooking a finger through the handle of his coffee cup and strode out of the room.

"Oh, Dr. Hunter! I didn't hear you call for me!" He heard Vivienne call as he passed her desk.

"I didn't call for you." He replied, not looking back.

"Well, would you like me to get you anything?" She asked.

"I am quite capable of fetching things for myself, Vivienne. I am not an invalid." His words came out a little harsher than he meant them to but he didn't apologise.

"Is there anything at all I can do for you?" She called after him stiffly. Great, now she was in a mood.

"Yes. Please make sure to take my messages for me while I'm gone."

"When will you be back?"

"I haven't decided yet." And he hadn't. At first, he'd only intended to go as far as the break room to make himself a cup of coffee and then head straight back to his desk. But now that he was out of the confines of his office, he felt a sudden rush of freedom. Maybe he'd go down and see some of his colleagues down in the labs. It'd been a while since he'd been down and annoyed Cole in person. As he headed towards the elevator, he remembered that he'd forgotten all about the coffee he wanted and was still carrying his empty mug. With a sigh, he turned away from the elevator and went to fetch the coffee.

Stood outside the break room, he could hear voices inside. He opened the door quietly and slipped inside, not wanting to disturb them. When most people saw him enter a room, their conversations would cease as if they feared that he would tell them off for gossiping or something. It was probably his own fault, he didn't participate in as many conversations with the staff as he supposed he should. He was probably making himself look more anti-social and unapproachable than they undoubtedly assumed he was. Maybe he should start making more of an effort.

He managed to slip into the room relatively unnoticed at any rate closing the door quietly behind him. There were two lab techs at the other end of the break room and they sat facing away from the door. The TV was on with a random news channel showing, but they didn't seem to be watching it. Discreetly filling the kettle from the tap, he listened in to their conversation.

"Did you hear Cole had a go at Ranford again?"

"What about this time?"

Jeremy sighed, it was well known that Dr. Cole and Dr. Ranford were both very opinionated and stubborn. Why they had chosen to work within the same project area was beyond him.

"He accused her of trying to fix his results so that hers would look better."

"Ugh. Sometimes they're no better than squabbling school children, I don't know why Dr. Hunter allows them to work together -"

"Comedic value?" Jeremy chipped in.

"-One of these days they're going to go too far and hurt each other." The other lab tech continued at the same time as Jeremy spoke. Both of them paused and looked around, their eyes widening when they caught sight of him.

"We're sorry, we didn't mean to..."

"It's perfectly fine. Everyone is entitled to their opinion." Jeremy shrugged.

"Really, we meant no harm..." The two of them jumped to their feet and started to leave but Jeremy raised his hands to stop them.

"There's no need for you to leave on my account." He smiled, "I was just making myself a cup of coffee." He raised it to show them, "And now I'm going back to my office. I was going to head down to see Dr. Cole, but if he's in one of those moods I don't think I shall bother."

The two lab techs chuckled, "Yeah, sometimes it's like world war three down there. It's a good job Dr. Renwells is down there to mediate half the time." Jeremy laughed as he thought of Dr. Ranford's ditzy assistant. It was true that she often managed to calm down her mentor. Maybe he ought to give her a bonus for it.

"Anyway ladies, I shall head back to work now. Good day and thanks for the heads up." He beamed at the two of them and headed out of the break room. He was glad that he'd managed to have a conversation – sort of – without the other participants running off in terror. Although he was sure that he was going to be the subject of gossip now. He could just imagine it: "Dr. Hunter spoke! And he was nice! I wonder if Viv's been putting anything in his coffee?"

When he finally sank back into the chair at his desk, he noticed that he had another email. First things first, he thought, leaning back in his chair and taking a satisfying sip of his coffee. Wasn't the first mouthful always the best? His mind drifted to the conversation he'd just overheard in the break room. If Cole and Ranford were getting on each other's nerves again he was going to have to go down there and make sure that they hadn't killed each other at some point. Maybe later this afternoon. Let them cool down a bit first.

Finally clicking on the email notification, he was pleasantly surprised to find that it was from Dominic. Ah, he had thought of an alternative. The idea of a forum was very intriguing. Perhaps Dominic would allow him to view it; he seemed to be a sort of kindred spirit, and from what his father had told him over the few times he'd spoken with him since the adoption, Dominic held an interest in science. If he could view the forum, it would help him to find out how the subjects were coping with their discovery – if they wished to disclose that to the others of course. And if they told the truth. The more he thought about the possibilities, the better it sounded. This forum, if they all found it, could become the main point of contact. Anything they wanted to talk about or plan could be done through this forum – it was an easy way for them to get to know each other without the vulnerability of actually meeting in person. Why hadn't he thought of this himself? Though, he supposed that if they knew he was watching; if anyone was watching, then they might be more reluctant to join up.

Gripping his coffee cup and smiling, he let his mind run over the possible outcomes. This should stop Cole and Ranford from killing each other for a little while at any rate. He wrote an emphatic yes back to Dominic, asking politely about discreetly being able to view the forum to aid in his research and wrote down the link to the forum so he could take it down to IT and ask them to add it in to the front page of his website for him.

Aaron Maysh

When Aaron woke the next morning, he hoped that the previous day had been a dream – well, more of a nightmare. That he wasn't adopted and part of some weird experiment.

"Aaron! Breakfast's ready!" His mother called as she heard him pad across his room to pull open his curtains and push the window open a tiny bit. Alright, so his mother was still running to the same routine. Maybe there was a chance it had been a dream after all.

"I'll be right down!" He called back, going to his wardrobe and picking out some clothes to wear. Pulling them on, he noticed a letter on his bedside table. His heart sank as he picked it up and saw the bold header on the folded side that was facing him confirming that yesterday had been very much real.

Sighing, he threw the letter to one side and headed downstairs for breakfast before his mother started calling for him again. Unlike yesterday, his brother was at the table eating, but his father was absent.

"Your father had to go to work early." His mother explained, noticing Aaron's glance to the empty chair. He nodded, although he didn't believe it. Was he really at work early, or had he just left so that he didn't have to face Aaron and could avoid the fact that Aaron had walked out last night and he'd had to come looking for him. If Reverend Jacobs was telling the truth then maybe his father was at the church praying away his sins. Maybe his father would pray to go back and never adopt him in the first place.

There seemed to be an awkwardness between Aaron and Jesse but their mother seemed not to notice. She chattered happily to the both of them, even if she didn't always get a reply. After putting the breakfast dishes into the dishwasher and clearing the table, Jesse had left the house quickly and Aaron returned to his room. The letter lay there in the middle of the floor, taunting and annoying him. There was something different about it since he'd seen it last night. Stooping to pick it up, whoever had left it in his room (he assumed his mother) had circled a website address.

Maybe it would help to look.

Was written underneath it. He'd recognise his mother's handwriting anywhere. As he sat and loaded his computer, he wondered whether his father knew that she was encouraging him to delve further into the science that had suddenly intruded on his life. Probably not. Carefully typing the website URL into the search bar, he waited for it to load but instead was met with a prompt window. It wanted a user name and password which he found printed on the back of the letter.

PLEASE LOG IN
USER NAME: 01AM
PASSWORD: KDTFJ48NSC

He entered the information given and clicked submit. The prompt vanished for a second before being replaced by another.

ENTER THE SITE.

Aaron clicked it and waited for the page to load. It was nothing out of the ordinary. Not overly fancy. Just a simple cream colour with an easy to follow layout. In the centre of the page at the top, there was a picture of a red-bricked building and underneath there was a list of various options.

He clicked on Project P.C.

PROJECT POPULATION CONTROL

Project P. C. was started in 1937 by Dr. Andrew Hunter. He believed that a population crisis was looming and took action to prevent it. If nothing is done to prevent accidental pregnancies, and to control and regulate the frequency of normal pregnancies, then the earth will find itself unable to cope. We shall have outgrown our planet as a population within 300 years! The team of scientists at Hunter and Sampson Science Enterprises strove to find a way to regulate the sex hormones, thus limiting the amount of viable sexual partners available and capping unexpected pregnancies. It would revolutionise birth control, no doubt providing a controversial conversation topic for many years to come.

An implant was developed. Small enough that it could be implanted into a human and be undetectable, the only trace of which would be a small scar hidden in the hair line. This implant is designed to utilise and regulate the necessary hormones for sexual awakening; puberty, and sexual intercourse itself.

As with most experiments intended for human use, Project P. C. was first undertaken using animal subjects. Starting out with basic laboratory rats, the project was deemed a success and worked its way up to using Primate subjects. These experiments, too, were a success. Unfortunately, their plans to progress to a human subject were released to the press and laboratories faced a huge public backlash. Picket lines formed outside the gates at all hours, trying to prevent anyone from taking a human into the lab to be tested on. Fortunately, a human infant had already been procured.

Raised in a predominantly scientific environment baby Adam (as the press later dubbed him), was watched with great trepidation until he reached the correct age to start puberty.

101

Imogen Chidwick

Tucked away in a comfortable corner of the library, Imogen was happily reading through one of her favourite books; Pride and Prejudice by Jane Austen. She had read it many, many times before always found herself coming back to it every couple of months.

It wasn't that other books weren't as good; she loved to read and was steadily working her way through both the teen fiction, and adult fiction sections of her local library. Newer books just didn't seem to be able to capture Imogen's heart and imagination like the older works. In large part, she was attracted to the romantic aspect of the old books, the way in which the characters went after the object of their affections. The language and writing style was also something she enjoyed. It was nicer, less brash than modern ways of writing.

Her friends told her that she was obsessed with them because she couldn't find herself a real boyfriend good enough to live up to the romantic expectations set forth by Mr. Darcy and the likes.

Since getting a letter explaining she was part of an experiment, she'd started to wonder if this was the reason behind her bad luck. The letter had also given her hope; somewhere out there was someone just for her. Someone who was going through the same thing she was and would understand her. It made her feel almost as though she was part of her own romance story.

As a familiar voice reached her ears, Imogen cursed herself for being a creature of habit. One of her friends had managed to track her down.

"Immo!" Susan practically shouted. Imogen thought about telling her to be quiet, but it wasn't really worth it. No doubt Susan had only ventured in to drag her outside, anyway.

"I thought I'd find you in here." Susan laughed, pulling up the front of Imogen's book so she could see the title. "Pride and Prejudice again? Haven't you read it a million times already?"

"It's a classic." Imogen shrugged.

"Whatever, anyway, I only came in here to drag you out for some lunch with us."

"I assumed as much." Imogen sighed, slipping her bookmark between the pages to mark her place and closing the book. She put it in her bag and rose to her feet.

"Giving up without a fight today?" Susan asked, surprised. Normally she had to whinge and moan for at least ten minutes before Imogen would deign to leave the library or whatever little nook she had found to read in.

"I'm hungry." Imogen smiled, "And it's easier to just go with you."

"You're damn right it is." Susan chatted away animatedly as they left the library and Imogen walked beside her quietly, nodding where appropriate. A couple of streets over, Susan led her into a small café where a table of their other friends waited. Imogen smiled politely, these were her friends from university and she hadn't seen them since the summer holidays started.

She exchanged the usual idle pleasantries; asking how everyone was and giving her own updates in return until it was time to decide what they wanted for dinner. Consulting the menu, Imogen was disappointed to find it sparse with vegetarian options and she silently cursed her friends for never remembering. In the end, she settled for an egg and cress sandwich, croissant and a black coffee. She waited politely for her friend's meals to arrive before starting her own. They had all ordered fried breakfasts, and Imogen fought against the urge to continue reading her book while they waited. It wasn't a huge wait in the end though, and she tucked into her food.

"So, what are your plans for the summer, Immo?" Tracy asked through a mouthful of bacon and beans.

"I hope you're not planning to spend the whole summer reading." Fiona laughed, as she dug through her bag to find a hair clip that would prevent her not-quite-long-enough fringe being covered in egg and grease.

"Actually, I was thinking joining my cousin on her holiday to the south of France for a few weeks." Imogen lied. She really had no intention of going anywhere, and although her cousin really was going to France, Imogen would only be going as far as Devon, having agreed to drive her cousin and her friend down to the ferry.

"What about you?" She asked.

It turned out that they were all going on holiday together and they had arranged this meet-up to try and coax Imogen into going with them so that she wouldn't be cooped up in a house reading by herself for an entire summer. Congratulating herself for thinking up an excuse just in case, Imogen professed her disappointment in not being able to go and promised them that next time they would all go on a trip together.

As soon as they had finished eating and Imogen felt that she could politely excuse herself, she did, rising from the table and headed towards the door.

"Oh, come on," Tracy called after her, "Surely you can stay a bit longer. We could have cake or something." Imogen turned back towards her friends but kept moving backwards towards the exit.

I really would love to stay, but I promised my mother I would help her this afternoon." Waving goodbye, Imogen turned around and found herself colliding with someone who had just entered the café.

"Sorry, love." Came a gruff reply, large hands gripped her arms as the man she'd bumped into steadied himself. Imogen recoiled from the contact immediately, pulling her arms out of his hands sharply before ducking round the man and all but running from the café. She ran blindly, eventually finding herself in a public toilet, locked safely inside a cubicle. Short of breath, she tried to push away the memories that had caused her to flee from the man in the café. But it was too late, the memory flooded her consciousness and she sank down on the toilet, head in her hands and cried.

Back in her first year of university she had gotten stupidly drunk at one of the dorm parties. In her naivety, she had trusted her friends to keep her safe, but instead they had pressured her into going back to Mark Hallam's room with him. He was the dorm's popular guy, and they had told her how stupid she would be if she didn't. Mark himself had threatened to spread horrid rumours about how she was a complete slut if she hadn't gone through with it.

Drunk, and with a slight attraction to Mark even though he was a jerk, Imogen had agreed. The hour that followed had been the worst of her life. It was painful and humiliating; Mark had mocked her and had left her there on the bed when he was done. Unable to tell anyone about what had happened, Imogen had transferred to a different university to get away from the people that had been her friends. She had made new, better friends at her new university. They never made jokes or probed about her distaste of physical contact. They had accepted her for who she was, and for that she was grateful. Now, having received that stupid letter, she wondered just how much of her life this experiment had affected.

Jennifer Dillon

Just when Jennifer thought her parents wouldn't be able to shock her any more than they had done in the past couple of days, they announced that they were going on holiday. A quiet weekend for the two of them to get away and reacquaint themselves. Ew.

"Thanks for the nightmares, mum!" She'd joked when they told her. Although her parents were apparently enough in love to go on holiday together they'd been having arguments for the past couple of days. This was something Jen was used to, having grown up around her parents sniping at each other all the time but this time something was different. If they were arguing and Jen entered the room they would shut up and stalk out. It was making her paranoid; what had she done that was causing arguments between her parents? It was driving her mad.

One day she'd come home from her part time waitressing job to find her mother reading a letter and sniffling. As soon as she realised Jen had seen her, she stuffed the letter into her pocket and quickly went to do something else before Jen could ask what was wrong. At least if they were going to be out of the house for the weekend she could have a good old snoop around. She'd learnt all of her mother's hiding places when she used to search for her Christmas presents. Once she reached a certain age she had learnt that if she didn't gloat and tell her mother she'd found her secret hiding place then she would be able to sneak a peek at all of her presents and her mother would unwittingly use the same hiding place the next year, and the next. It was almost a given; and every child's dream.

Unfortunately, her parents weren't leaving until tomorrow morning, and the urge to seek out the letter was driving her wild. The thought clawed at her mind every time she passed her mother's favourite hiding place, but she was too afraid to look in case she was caught and her mother took the letter on holiday with them. Then she would never get to see it!

And so, she waited. Biding her time by working, and visiting Sam. Even offering to help her mother pack later that day. Anything to bring her one step closer to knowing what the hell was going on. It also meant that she could make sure her mother didn't pack any suspicious looking letters. She didn't have to worry about her father, he'd always been useless with keeping important information and relied heavily on her mother to help him.

Ethan Foy

Ethan glanced up at the clock for what had to be the millionth time. Ten minutes till closing. That wasn't so bad. At one point, he'd been convinced that the clock had been stuck on quarter past four for the last couple of hours.

It had been a slow day; very few customers had been in and the time had just dragged by. He'd even asked the managed if they could close up early, but she'd told him no. To try and kill the last hour of work, Ethan had taken to rotating the stock and refilling dwindling supplies.

It was only a small shop; it sold most forms of stationary, from tiny erasers up to giant Art folders, and it had a photocopy and binding section in the back. Because it was so small, the stock was kept in the cellar, and heading up and down the stairs to retrieve new stock was part of the reason Ethan had chosen to do that particular job; it was a great time waster.

Molly, Ethan's best friend and co-worker, was helping him replenish the packs of paper. It was something they sold a lot of because of their proximity to local offices and the town college. If they ever ran short of paper for printing or photocopying, they'd come to the store and purchase a couple of reams.

"So how's it going with Stacy?" Molly asked as they heaved another heavy box of paper up the stairs to the store.

"Broke it off." Ethan grunted in reply, he was on the bottom and carrying most of the weight.

"Why? I thought you liked this one."

"It wasn't working out."

"What was wrong with her?"

"Nothing."

"So why wasn't it working?"

Ethan sighed, he hated that Molly probed so deeply into his relationships sometimes. He valued her friendship, but she was the nosiest person he knew.

"It wasn't her."

"Oh that old treasure." Molly mocked, "It's not you, it's me."

"It really was though. I just wasn't interested in her."

"Well you seemed pretty interested last week."

"Things change."

"Just another notch on your belt, huh?"

"Can we just stop talking about this?" Ethan groaned. Molly remained silent, and Ethan thought he had won, for the time being. He knew that the questions would begin again though. They always did with Molly.

"So if it wasn't her that was the problem, why are you so down in the dumps?" She asked, right on cue as they reached the shop floor and put down the box. Ethan turned his back on her and started to stack the paper in the boxes by the entrance. After a couple of minutes, Molly sighed. She knew she wasn't going to get an answer just yet, not until Ethan was ready to give her one.

"So how about we go out tonight?" She asked.

"You're asking me out?" Ethan turned to look at her.

"No!" She blurted, a little too quickly for Ethan's liking. "I mean just as mates. You and me."

"I don't know..."

"Aw, come on Eth, it'll be great fun."

Ethan picked up the now empty crate and started towards the door to the cellar. "Can I pick the film?" He asked, remembering that there was a zombie film out that he had been meaning to go and see.

"Of course!" Molly beamed.

"Alright then. It's a date." Ethan winked at her before disappearing into the cellar.

"I can't believe you made me watch that rubbish!" Molly complained as they entered the Chinese restaurant after the movie.

"Hey, you said I could pick the film." Ethan laughed. It really had been terrible; a low budget zombie film with bad actors and even worse sound-editing. It was no wonder only a selected few cinemas were showing it nationwide.

"I didn't realise you'd be picking such a crap one!"

"It was funny though."

"I think you need to look up the definition of funny." Molly shot back, laughing. "If it had been funny, it might have redeemed itself a tiny bit." She held up her finger and thumb with the tiniest fraction of a space between the two of them as she said it. Their conversation was interrupted as they were shown to their seats and ordered their drinks. Ethan ordered a pint of lager, while Molly went for a rum and coke. For a moment, Ethan thought about mocking her for her girly choice in beverages but thought better of it. Knowing Molly wouldn't hesitate to kick him beneath the table.

A couple of drinks and a Pork Chow Mein each later, it was time to leave the restaurant. While they were eating, it had started to rain, so they huddled together in the doorway of a nearby building while Ethan rang a taxi.

"Ten minutes." He smiled down at Molly, who was huddled close to his side to avoid the rain, practically using him as an umbrella. She nodded, having to look up to be able to meet his gaze. Her hair was damp, and a little out of place, making Ethan chuckle to himself before reaching down and moving a strand of hair from her cheek.

His hand lingered there a little too long, and in his almost drunken haze, Ethan realised that he wanted to kiss Molly. How could it have been that she had been here the whole time and he hadn't noticed her like this before? She was beautiful. He wondered whether his problems keeping girls was because he hadn't found the right one yet. And Molly had said so herself on previous occasions; what if she was trying to show him that she was the one?

Leaning in, he pressed his lips to hers, tasting salt and alcohol as she kissed him back for a second before pulling away fast.

"Ethan, don't." She looked away.

"Why not?" He asked, confused and hurt.

"Because you're my best friend, it'll ruin everything."

"No it wouldn't, I can't see why we haven't done this before now."

Molly sighed and moved away from him. "You just don't get it."

"Get what?"

"I like you, Ethan." Now he really was confused, if she liked him what was the problem? He looked at her until she continued. "You have a reputation. One that I've seen myself."

"What are you talking about?"

"You date a girl a couple of times and then you break it off. I don't want to be just another failed relationship, Ethan. It would be better if we just stayed friends." Was that really what he was like? Of course it was, he scowled. His mind flicked to the letter he'd been trying to ignore and wondered if that was the source of his problem.

"I'm sorry Molly. You're right."

"Let's just forget about it, ok?" Ethan nodded and stepped forwards as the taxi finally pulled up at the side of the road.

"You take it, I think I'm going to walk." He told Molly as he opened the door and watched her slide in. She turned to protest, but Ethan was already gone.

Jennifer Dillon

Today was the day! Jen's parents were finally going on holiday so she was just hours away from finding out what the hell had been going on. She jumped out of bed, showered and got dressed. After breakfast she slouched on the sofa in the front room trying to act casual, making conversation with her father about their trip. She asked whether they had packed everything, what the weather was going to be like, and told him make sure to bring her back something cool. Which would probably just end up being a keyring that she could add to her collection.

After what seemed like forever, it was finally time for her parents to leave, so Jen shoved her feet into some shoes and went out to help them pack the car.

"Jeeze, you know you're only going for the weekend!" She huffed as she hauled her mother's suitcase into the boot.

"Well, you can never be too prepared!" Her mother replied a little haughtily. Jen rolled her eyes and her father laughed.

"It's a good job we aren't flying, just think of the extra baggage charge we'd have to pay!" Her father teased.

"Would you prefer I walked around naked the whole time?"

"Well, there's an idea..."

"Ew. Over share. I'll bill you for the therapy, Dad." Jen made a face. Somehow, they had managed to fit everything in the boot and get it closed.

"Now, you know the rules." Her mother opened the door before turning towards Jen.

"Yeah, yeah. No parties, no strangers, no breaking anything. The only person who'll even possibly be coming round is Sam. And Grandma if you've been talking to her behind my back again."

"Mum!" She cried at the shifty look that had followed the previous statement, "I'm twenty years old, I can look after myself! I don't need Grandma checking in on me."

"I know that honey, but she hasn't seen you in a while. I thought it would be nice, plus she'll want to check on your sisters as well."

Jen frowned. Although. Perhaps her Grandma would know something about what was going on. Her mother still confided in her a lot, so she should have been privy to at least some of the conversations Jen always managed to interrupt. Eventually her mother stopped fussing. Yes, she had all the emergency numbers. Yes, she had the hotel's number just in case. Yes, she knew the hours she was working. Yes, she would remember to feed herself and make sure her sister fed the twins and not burn the house down. Yes to a dozen more stupid questions.

She could barely contain herself when the car pulled out of the driveway. Waving like a loon for as long as she could see her mother waving back at her. As soon as the car was out of sight she raced into the house and headed straight for her mother's secret place. It was in her wardrobe. Or rather under it. There was a panel of wood that ran beneath the doors, and if you knocked the left-hand side of it, it came away easily. Jen had discovered it completely by accident one day when she had been playing and knocked it off.

Afraid she'd be told off, Jen had simply pushed the piece of wood back and run out of her mother's room. The secret place had slipped from her young mind until later on in the year when she spotted a ribbon poking out from underneath it. She had pulled the wood away again; first making sure that her mother was still in the back garden hanging out the washing in the rare winter sunshine and had been over the moon when she found toys!

114

There were rolls of wrapping paper under there as well, and it hadn't taken her long to figure out that these were Christmas presents for her and her sisters. In quite possibly the smartest moment of her life, she'd kept quiet about finding the presents. And her mother had continued to use the same place year after year meaning that she got to play with all of her sister's toys before they did.

She ran to her mother's room now and pulled away the piece of wood. Nothing. Well, unless you counted the dust bunny colony currently squatting in there. Frowning, she pushed the piece of wood back into place. Since she and her sisters had all grown up, her mother obviously didn't need to use the hidey-hole anymore.

Collapsing onto her mother's bed for a moment, she looked around the room. There were numerous draws that she could have stuffed the letter into. If it was even hidden in here. Maybe it was somewhere else in the house.

Twenty-four hours, and three ransacked rooms later, Jen had found what she hoped was the suspicious letter. It wasn't about rent owed, or council tax, or water rates or any of the other household things that her mother seemed to hoard letters about. This one was from some laboratory she'd never heard of. Jen's eyes widened in shock and confusion as she read it, and she almost dropped it. Was this what her parents had been keeping from her? That she was some science freak they'd adopted out of pity? It couldn't be either of her sisters because they weren't old enough. And now her parents had conveniently gone on holiday, so she couldn't even ask them if it was true.

How could have they never bothered to tell her that she was adopted. What if this was why her parents had split up in the first place? What if they had argued over who would tell her? If they had, she hoped that it was her dad that would've wanted to tell her. Somehow that made her feel better. Stuffing the letter into her back pocket, Jen fled the house, only just remembering to grab the keys and lock up as she left. The mess could stay as it was for all she cared. Right now, she needed to see her grandmother.

Aaron Maysh

Curiosity kept dragging Aaron back to the HSSE website. There was never anything new to find there, and he must have read through every page over a dozen times. He also knew the names of practically every member of staff that was listed on the website and could describe them from their pictures.

Today, though, something had changed. On the main page, beneath the introduction there was a link that hadn't been there before. Like a black mark on a white piece of paper his eyes were drawn straight to it. It was just two words. Soul Echo. And he could only tell it was a link because it became underlined when he moved his mouse over it. After a couple of seconds of hesitation, he clicked and waited as he was redirected to a new page. It looked like a forum. There was only one thread in it at the moment called Introductions, and Aaron could see from the menu it had a couple of replies.

Aaron looked it at it, intrigued. Did this mean that some of the others had also found their way here? He took his hand away from the mouse as if it was going to bite him. Did he really want to get into this? If he looked in there and saw the others' posts then there'd be no turning back. Absolutely no chance at all of turning his back on this whole science experiment thing. He'd be in it for the long haul. Taking a deep breath, he decided to do it. After all the main website said that one of those nine people was his intended partner. Maybe even his future wife if things went that far.

Taking the mouse again, he clicked the Introductions thread but was denied entry. This time he was asked to create a user name and password before he could go any further. After some thought, he decided to go with MonsterMaysh after one of his favourite songs combined with a play on his name. Now that he had signed up properly, he clicked the introductions thread again, pleasantly surprised when it opened.

INTRODUCTIONS
Posted by **D0M1N1C**

Hi. I'm not sure if any of you will ever actually read this, but I am also a part of Project P. C. According to my letter, I am #04. I made this forum in the hopes that we could all get to know each other but remain as anonymous as we each wished to. This forum is not publicly accessible, so any personal information posted here will only be visible to us 10.

A little about me:

My name is Dominic, which you may have already gathered from my oh-so imaginative user name. I am 20 (aren't we all!) and currently at home for the summer holidays. When I am not at home I study Computer Sciences and Physics at University. I look forward to getting to know anyone else that decides they would also like to post.

~Dominic.

RE: INTRODUCTIONS
Posted by **Candi.**

Hey!

Wow, It's so great to finally see proof that there are other people involved! I was beginning to think my parents had tried to pull some stupid practical joke on me or something. I'm Cam. My letter says I'm #03. Does that mean I'm one better than you? LOL. I am also staying with my parents for the summer hols, although we are on holiday at the moment (yay!).

RE: INTRODUCTIONS

Posted by **Flipside**

Hey guys. My name's Helen, and according to my letter I am #08. I'm kinda surprised only two of you have posted so far, I thought for sure that I would be the last person to find out!

I am also away from Uni for the summer, but I'm not going to be home for long. There's a great summer sports camp I go to every year. I'm obsessed with surfing and do a little bit of skateboarding too. I doubt anyone else from here will be going, the world's not that small is it? Camp's a couple weeks long, so I won't be around for a while - there's no internet access available.

Catch you on the flip side!

Helen.

Aaron read through the posts a few times. The others had all given away their first names but there was no way they could be tracked down just from that, was there? Even though he'd signed up to the forum, he still wasn't sure he was going to actually post until he was clicking the reply button. This was it. There was no going back now.

Helen Askew

"Yes, brill! Alright Brian, I'll see you then. Byyyeee!" Helen put the phone down, smiling having just scored herself three weeks paid work at Haversham Lodge – a sports adventure camp that ran every summer in Yorkshire. All throughout school Helen had attended as a camper. This year, however, she was too old to be a camper, so she had used her initiative and checked to see if the camp needed any Leaders this year; young adults who were responsible for overseeing cabins of children, taking part in their activities and generally making sure they had a good time.

Originally, Helen had missed the sign-up date and was put on a reserves list. As luck would have it, one of the girls who had signed up on time broke her leg in a skiing accident so the camp was down a female Leader. Helen had jumped at the chance. As soon as she was done on the phone to Brian, she pulled a notebook and pen towards her and started to make a list of things she would need to take with her – most of which, she'd already have, she just had to dig it out of her mum's garage.

Brian had told her that she was free to arrive any time from today as long as it was before the end of the week, so she was eager to get packed and ready to go. Before she could put pen to paper her phone rang again. This time it was her mother. Great.

"Helen, darling!" Her mother bellowed down the phone. No matter how many times Helen told her that she didn't need to shout to be heard, the bloody woman refused to listen. Was it an age thing?

"Good morning to you, too, Mum." She replied, tucking the phone between her ear and her shoulder before starting to write her list.

"I was just calling to invite you over for lunch." Her mother trilled, "You haven't been over in ages, and I know you have some free time now." Helen sighed and quickly explained about the camp offering her a Leader position for two weeks. Three including set up week.

"Well darling that's all the more reason for you to come over for lunch. Come on, it'll only be a small one."

"Mum, I really have to get packing."

"Oh, you have plenty of time! I know you'll just throw everything in a bag anyway. I'll be expecting you at one o'clock sharp."

Helen considered it, though she knew she really didn't have a choice unless she wanted to hear about this for the rest of her life. It was only ten, she could probably have everything packed and ready to go by one. And, on the plus side, if she went to see her mother now she'd be off the hook for visiting for at least a week or two after camp finished.

"Alright fine, I'll see you at one." Helen hung up midway through the delighted squeal that followed and read through her list. It looked as though she had pretty much everything she needed already. She was only missing a few things, camp essentials like face wipes and bug spray and she'd easily be able to pick those up somewhere along the way.

As she headed out to the hall closet to fetch her rucksack, Helen caught sight of her reflection in the hallway mirror and paused. Her shoulder-length, raven black hair was messy and wild, swirling about her head like a bird's nest where she'd been playing with it when she'd been on the phone to Brian earlier. Laughing at herself, she pulled her hair up into a messy bun, tying it with a hair bobble she had around her wrist before retrieving her rucksack.

An hour and a half later, Helen had squashed as much as she physically could into her rucksack as she possibly could and was

121

pondering the idea of taking another bag. When you were a mere camper, there was a limit of one large bag per person. Mostly because as a kid you could barely carry that. Now that she was a Leader maybe there'd be a bit more leeway and besides, even if there was still a one bag rule, she was allowed to take her car and she could easily stash an extra bag in her boot.

Having managed to narrow it down to just two bags, Helen tucked them away in the boot of her car and climbed into the driver's seat. It was almost one and her mother was expecting her for lunch. If she didn't get there soon she could expect a very frantic phone call from an upset mother thinking she'd been abandoned. Helen rolled her eyes at the thought and started the car.

"Mum, I'm here!" Helen called as she opened the door.

"In here, darling!" Her mother called from the living room. She could hear her mother talking to someone in hushed tones and wondered who it was. As she got closer, she realised it was a guy and her guard rose instantly. So, her mother's innocent invitation for lunch was really another attempt to set her up with some single son of a colleague, or a friend? She should have known there'd be an ulterior motive for this.

In the seconds it took to walk from the front door to the living room, Helen had already considered several excuses that she could use to escape from this awful situation. It wasn't the first time her mother had pulled a sneaky trick like this and Helen was sure that it wouldn't be the last either, her mother was constantly on the lookout for a suitable boyfriend to provide for her.

Helen thought the whole thing was laughable. As if she wanted to be tied down to someone like that. She considered herself a free spirit, and the fact that she'd never had a boyfriend that lasted longer than a week didn't bother her in the slightest. She knew that her mother wanted grandchildren but the thought of being a housewife was Helen's idea of a nightmare. She'd settle down when she was ready.

"There you are." Her mother smiled and rose to her feet as Helen entered the living room, her voice overly pleasant and fake sounding, which made Helen grit her teeth. The mystery boy by her side also stood. "I have someone I'd like to introduce you to." She gestured to the boy and smiled, confirming Helen's suspicions that this wouldn't be a normal lunch.

"This is Tyler."

The boy – Tyler – stepped forwards and offered his hand. "It's very nice to meet you." He smiled, and Helen felt sorry for him as she took his hand in greeting. He was attractive; she had to give him that, handsome compared to some of the other prospective husbands her mother had paraded her in front of. Tyler was tall and lean, with sky blue eyes, scruffy brown hair and dimples when he smiled. If Helen had met him out somewhere, maybe she would have given him a chance.

"It's lovely to meet you, too." Helen smiled as politely as she could. Poor guy. How long had he been stuck here talking to her mother? How had she even roped him into this?

"Can I get you a cup of tea?" Her mother asked.

"No, thanks. I'll get myself a glass of water."

"Helen, darling, I insist." Her mother stressed the words darling and insist, pulling her into the room by her wrist and pushing her towards Tyler. Subtlety had never been her mother's strong point.

"I can fetch my own drink." Helen protested through her teeth, but her mother had already left the room. Helen did her best to control her temper as she dropped into the chair next to Tyler.

"So how do you know my mother?" She asked politely, wondering how she was going to escape. She felt a bit bad for Tyler though, poor guy had come here expecting to meet a girl he might end up getting a date out of, and he'd gotten her instead.

"She knows my mum through the community centre."

"Ah, I see. Yours is into blind dates too huh?"

Tyler laughed. "Yeah, something like that." He blushed and nervously ran a hand through his hair and reached into his back pocket for something. "Actually, your mum gave my mum a picture of you." He held it out and Helen took it, looking down at her own smiling face before folding the picture in half and stuffing it in her own pocket. Her mother had gone too far this time.

Now Helen felt awful about her plans to escape. "Oh, right." That had thrown her off guard; she wasn't sure what else to say. He'd obviously come because he thought she was attractive. Or his mother was as pushy as her own. Maybe it was both. An awkward silence settled heavily between them. Luckily her mother chose that moment to bustle in carrying Helen's glass of water and a tray of sandwiches.

She took the water gladly and took a long sip. Her mind still focused on getting out of the house, Helen didn't notice her mother's frantic looks back and forth between her and Tyler.

"So where is it that you work, Tyler?" Her mother asked, obviously trying to open a conversation between the two of them.

"My dad owns a bathroom salesroom, I work there." He smiled, reaching forwards and taking a sandwich. As her mother replied, Helen had an idea. The bathroom! Of course, why hadn't she thought of it before?

"If you'll excuse me," She smiled politely, "I'll just be a minute" Her mother looked up at her, outraged that she was trying to leave the room until Helen mouthed 'bathroom' at her.

"Hurry back, darling." She smiled. Helen nodded and exited the living room.

As soon as she was safely in the bathroom, Helen shut the door and locked it. Crossing to the window, she unlatched it and pushed. The window was on the ground floor, so the fall would be barely anything, and it was big enough for her to squeeze through. Unfortunately, it was locked. She pushed again, double checking, but it was definitely locked.

"Shit shit shit." Helen racked her brains trying to remember where the key would be. Hadn't she used it herself a million times before she's moved out? She checked in all the weird little pots and useless ornaments on the windowsill before opening the cabinet above the sink and checking in there. By the time she reached last shelf in the cabinet, Helen was getting desperate. If she didn't find the key soon she'd have to go back out there and make more small talk and probably be forced to agree to a date just to get her mother off her back. She'd already been in the bathroom for long enough.

Closing the cabinet with a defeated sigh, Helen caught the reflection of the wall behind her in the mirrored front. There, right next to the window, was a little hook with a tiny key ring holding two keys. How the hell had she missed them before?

"Idiot." She scolded herself, but it didn't matter now, she had her escape route. As quietly as she could, she pushed the key into the lock, turned it and pushed the window wide open. Taking another few seconds to carefully move all her mother's ornaments to the other side of the windowsill – why did she have so bloody many - Helen unlocked the bathroom door and clambered onto the toilet seat.

A moment later, she was on the ground and sneaking around the side of the house. She kept low so that her mother and poor Tyler wouldn't see her through the window. Unfortunately, her mother had a gravel driveway, and though Helen did her best to traverse it quietly she couldn't be sure.

Thankful that she hadn't bothered to lock her car, Helen opened the door and squeezed through as small a gap as she could manage. With the door still open, she did up her seat belt and slid her key into the ignition knowing that as soon as she started the car she'd be caught.

Taking a deep breath, Helen shut the door, started the car and reversed out of the driveway. As her rear tyres left the pavement and hit the road, Helen saw her mother standing in the open doorway with her hands on her hips. Tyler, standing behind her, looked amused and Helen couldn't help but give them both a small wave as she turned into the street, put the car into gear and drove off. She'd never hear the end of it, she knew. But it had been so worth it to see the look on her mother's face.

Camilla Everett

Cam swiped the shower-steamed mirror, with a flannel, scrutinising her reflection with pursed lips and narrowed eyes. She had high, delicate cheek bones, warm blue eyes, a perfectly sculpted nose that led down into plump, pink lips. Her hair was long, and two shades of blonde lighter than her perfect eyebrows.

It wasn't her face that she was unhappy with. It was her breasts. She agonised daily over the size of them, comparing them to all the other women she saw around her; her mother, friends, strangers, models. She was twenty years old, and there were fourteen-year olds out there with better developed breasts than she would ever had.

Scowling, she turned away from the mirror, allowing it to steam up again as she continued her morning shower. As the soap suds slid down the barely-there-curves of her boyish form, Cam decided to get together a group of her friends and go shopping. Retail therapy always made her feel better.

Finishing up in the shower, Cam wrapped herself in a fluffy yellow towel, wrung out her hair and padded through to her bedroom. Picking out her prettiest padded bra and some matching underwear from the chest of drawers by her bed, Cam flung open the door of her walk-in wardrobe and tried to decide what she would wear today. In the end she decided on a pretty summer dress; designed to look more like a top and skirt than a one-piece dress. It was knee length, black and white stripes on the top, and navy blue on the bottom, separated in the middle by a black belt. Taking the clothes back into her bedroom she dried herself off and dressed quickly. Tucking her feet into a pair of fluffy, white slippers, Cam danced over to her phone, hoping that her friends wouldn't be too busy to join her on a shopping spree today.

After an hour Cam had managed to coerce five of her friends into dropping what they were doing and going on a shopping trip. Satisfied, she blow-dried and styled her hair, considered changing her outfit a couple of times and changed everything she needed into the right handbag before slipping on a pair of strappy sandals and leaving her house.

She'd barely found a place to park in the multi-storey when her mobile was buzzing in her handbag. Rolling her eyes at her friends' impatience, she dug around for it and put it between her ear and shoulder as she finished parking, her wing mirror getting dangerously close to a steel beam.

"Hey Laura."

"Cam, where are you?"

"I'm just parking; I'll be there in a minute. Patience is a virtue, you know." She wasn't even as late as she usually was. Fifteen minutes was barely anything.

"I'll have you know that I've got a cousin called Patience and she's far from virtuous."

Cam chuckled; Laura could never stand to be patient. She had a maximum waiting time of two minutes; three on a good day. Saying goodbye to Laura, Cam fetched a ticket for her car and headed down to meet her friend. When she reached the café where they'd arranged to meet Laura was already tapping her foot.

"Am I the first to arrive?" Cam asked, genuinely shocked.

"Do you see anyone else?" Laura snapped.

"Well do you want to go and get a coffee while we wait?"

"I guess so."

For a moment Cam regretted inviting Laura because she had a habit of being snappy like this, but she was also the only person that could ever be counted on to arrive on time. The other four were nowhere to be seen and they were almost twenty minutes late now. In the end, it took another half an hour for all four of them to finally show up. And by this time Laura wasn't the only person that was annoyed.

"What time do you call this?" Cam demanded. "We were supposed to meet up earlier."

"We stopped for some food on the way over, it's no big deal."

"No big deal? We've been waiting for over half an hour. And it was nice of you to see if we wanted anything to eat."

The girl in the middle, Sharon, rolled her eyes and smirked. "Oh please, we all know that neither of you eat to keep it down."

"Whatever let's just get going." Cam sighed. She had once been bulimic, but counselling had helped her through it. And no matter how many times she asked Sharon to stop mentioning it, she would always be ignored. Giving a slight nod to Laura, Cam rose from her chair and took her empty coffee cup to the counter. With Laura following behind her, they left the coffee shop, not bothered whether Sharon, Liz, Danielle and Tasha were coming with them. She honestly didn't care if they did or not.

The first couple of shops passed in a blur of mindless conversation and boring clothes. Cam had found nothing she wanted to try on and was becoming increasingly annoyed at the snail pace Sharon and the others had set behind her. In the next shop, however, she found plenty of clothes to try on. She and her friends went around the shop twice before deciding to head into the changing room to try a few things on.

Trying on the first top, Cam was glad that she'd decided to wear a padded bra today. It made her feel a lot better about her reflection and how she looked in it. Without padding it would simply hang there, limp and lifeless. As she pulled the top over her head to try on the next one, Sharon poked her head into the cubicle.

"What do you think of this- oh, sorry Cam!" She laughed, backing out of the cubicle as Cam quickly pulled down her top to hide her body. Taking deep breaths and counting to three, Cam changed into the next top and poked her head out to reply to Sharon. But she wasn't there.

Wandering further down the row of cubicles, Cam looked for Sharon. Eventually she heard her voice coming from a cubicle. The curtain was drawn across the doorway and she was talking to Danielle and Liz.

"Don't you think I look great in this top?" She asked, posing in front of the mirror. Cam peeked through the gap between the curtain and the wall; it was the same top she had been trying on when Sharon had barged in on her.

"It makes my boobs look great." She continued when the two girls nodded their agreement.

"Your boobs always look great." Liz simpered, and Cam rolled her eyes. That was Liz, ever the kiss-ass.

"Yeah, a lot better than some peoples." Danielle offered.

Sharon chuckled, "You mean our friend in the padded bra?" Liz and Danielle giggled, and Sharon continued, "I mean really, you call those boobs? They're more like tic-tacs on an ironing board!"

Cam's heart sank as the three girls in the cubicle dissolved into fits of giggles. They were supposed to be her closest friends, yet here they were mocking her behind her back. A red-hot flash of anger spread through her and she steeled herself for what she was about to do. Drawing back the curtain, she took pleasure in the shock that spread across their faces, killing the laughter in its tracks.

"Cam... we were just talking about my..." Sharon stuttered.

"I heard what you were talking about."

"We didn't mean anything by it, it was just a joke..." Sharon was cut off mid-sentence as Cam slapped her hard across the face.

"Sorry, just joking!" She spat at Sharon as she raised a hand to cover her red face, tears blooming in her eyes. "It's all just a bit of fun, remember." She added. "Maybe we should all laugh about how you wet the bed until you were eleven? Or about how your moustache is showing?"

Liz and Danielle said nothing, both had taken a step away from Sharon and stood with their hands over their mouths and their eyes open wide. Tuning on her heel, Cam went back to her own cubicle; changed into her original top and left the clothes she had been trying on hanging in the hook. A sales assistant would find them eventually.

Grabbing her handbag, Cam stormed down the row of cubicles, not even bothering to look in on Sharon, Liz and Danielle as she thundered past. Laura was nowhere to be seen. Cam kept up her thunderous pace until she got to her car, where she sat behind the steering wheel and took a few deep breaths. Reversing out while she was in such a mood would probably result in a dented bumper; or worse. After counting to ten she felt calm enough to reverse out and leave the car park.

She knew that Laura would be annoyed that she had vanished, but she'd call her later and explain. Not to mention find out what Sharon and the others had told her too. As if she were on autopilot, Cam found herself on a route that headed further into town rather than away from it and towards home. It wasn't until she arrived that she realised where she had driven. Halberk's. Founded by Alana Halberk, it was an all-female surgery group that specialised in breast reconstruction. It was mainly for women that had recovered from breast cancer, but they also did cosmetic cases.

Cam had often thought about getting breast enlargement surgery, but she could never find the courage. Every now and then she would wind up outside the surgery and sit peering through the window, clutching the steering wheel until her knuckles turned white and criticising herself for being such a coward. She would see other women coming and going from the surgery, marvelling at how happy they looked whenever they were leaving, and imagining herself in their position.

For now, though, she was still a coward. Sighing, she pulled back out into the road and started the drive towards home.

Ethan Foy

"I've just got to shut down my PC, then I'll be ready." Ethan promised his mum. She was getting ready to go for a long weekend away with some of her girlfriends, but she couldn't leave until Ethan had gone because his car was blocking hers in the driveway.

Sitting down at his computer, Ethan looked at the open web page. Soul Echo. It wasn't the first time he'd visited the site, but it was the first day he'd logged in using the account he'd made. He opened the only thread in there and had a read through the other introductions. Most of the others had posted by now, but he knew he wasn't the last one to do so.

One of the entries half way down the page caught his eye. It was by a girl named Helen who was going away to a summer sports camp. Ethan was also heading to a sports camp, but it couldn't possibly the same one, could it? He thought about sending her a message out of curiosity, but if they were headed to the same camp then there was a chance that she might already be on her way and not see his message until afterwards.

If only she'd posted a picture of herself, he could have kept any eye out for her. He was still going to try and track her down though, and seeing as he was quite popular at camp, it wouldn't be too much of a hassle for him to get hold of the camp roster. It narrowed it down a lot more knowing that she was his age, so she had to be a leader like him.

Glancing up at the clock, he realised he didn't have time to send her a message anyway. As he shut down the computer, he received an email from his girlfriend Chloe, but he didn't have time to stay and read it. If he got lucky, maybe there'd be a bit of signal and he could read it on his phone once he got to camp. She'd probably think he was avoiding her or something, which was true, since he'd received the letter he'd spent more time avoiding her than with her and he was surprised that she hadn't just broken up with him already. Hearing a shout from his mother telling him to hurry up, Ethan ran down the stairs two at a time, wondering if he would find this girl at camp, and what he would say if he did.

Grabbing his bag and kissing his mother, Ethan ran out of the front door. Orientation was in a couple of hours, and if he missed it he'd be in big trouble. He could also miss his first opportunity to find Helen; all the Leaders had to attend orientation, so they could be signed up to activities to run and partnered with another Leader.

As he started up his car, Ethan thought about how great it would be if this Helen girl was not only going to the same camp but ended up being his partner as well. Pulling out of the drive, Ethan waved to his mother and sped off. He had to find her. Maybe they were meant to be.

Jennifer Dillon

"What's wrong, child?" Jen's Grandmother asked as she opened her front door to find her hysterical granddaughter there clutching at a letter.

Jen thrust the letter towards her. "Tell me you didn't know."

"Come now, sit down and let me see what's gotten you into this state."

Jen allowed her grandmother to steer her into the living room and sank into the sofa. Her grandmother had vanished, and Jen could hear clinking in the kitchen; she was making them both a cup of tea. Her Gran's cups of tea were magical, and she knew it'd make her feel better. Still, her eyes lingered on the crumpled letter that had been abandoned on the coffee table in front of her.

"Now Jennifer. What's all this about?" Her Grandmother asked, raising her cup to her mouth and taking a delicate sip. She still had not touched the letter. Jen glared at it for a moment hoping she would catch on, but nothing. Her Gran just watched her, waiting for an answer.

"Did you know I was adopted?"

"Of course." She took another sip. "Your mother was very excited about the whole thing."

"So, you know where they got me from. You know I'm part of some freak experiment?" Her grandmother paused and finally put her cup of tea down. Jennifer was holding hers tightly between her hands but hadn't drank any of it.

"Now, that part I didn't know. Is that what you are so upset about?" Trust Grandma to be so calm in the face of news like that.

Jen motioned to the letter. "I found that at home. It's dated a couple of days before I came home. Mum and Dad knew this whole time and never said a word!" she waited patiently, finally giving in and drinking her own tea as her Grandmother read through the letter. Honestly, what did she put in it? As the warmth spread through her, Jen was already feeling better.

"Yes. I can see how much this would upset you." Jen nodded and opened her mouth to speak but her Grandmother cut her off. "I'm sure that your parents had a very good reason to keep this from you. But it doesn't change the fact that they love you. And it definitely doesn't change the fact that I love you."

Jen sighed. Grandma was supposed to take her side! To comfort her and tell her everything was going to be okay, and that she had have words with her daughter when she returned from their holiday.

"You should talk to them when they come home. It seems you have much to sort out." Gran told her. Jen nodded. When had her Grandmother become such a pacifist? She had always stood up for Jen, but now it seemed she was making her stand up for herself, which quite frankly, sucked.

Bonnie Kinsella

Precariously balancing a coffee in one hand, and her mobile phone, keys and breakfast in the other, Bonnie pushed open the doors that led into the foyer of the building she worked in. As she was almost all the way through, a passing man took pity on her and held the door open.

"Thank you!" She called over her shoulder as she followed a small crowd towards the elevator. She wasn't in a hurry, but her colleagues would be in soon, and she wanted to eat her breakfast without being moaned at for not bringing something for everyone in her office. They were only a small team of five, so sometimes they would take it in turns to buy breakfast for everyone.

Putting everything carefully onto her desk, Bonnie slipped into her chair and turned on her ancient computer so that by the time she'd finished eating her breakfast it'd be just about ready for her to use. Management reasoned that she didn't need a high-tech computer just for data entry and wouldn't fork out the dough to get her a new one. Instead she got everyone else's second-hand units when they got their own new ones. They were right, of course, but having a PC that didn't take over fifteen minutes to load would be loads better. And it would make the day much more fun if she could check her emails from work without having to use the simplest form of the web page possible.

Just as she was depositing the wrappings from her breakfast into the bin and pushing it back under her desk with her foot, the first of Bonnie's colleagues arrived.

"You're here early." George smiled, taking his seat opposite Bonnie and turning on his slightly less ancient computer.

"The train was on time for once." She lied. The train was always on time, it's just that some mornings she preferred to eat breakfast in the café and sometimes it was too busy to do that, so she ended up eating it in the office.

"You're in a good mood, today." George commented, pulling a banana from his satchel and peeling it.

"Today's my last day." Bonnie grinned, "My holiday starts tomorrow."

"How could I forget?" George laughed, "You've only reminded us every day for the past two weeks." Bonnie crumpled a piece of paper and threw it at George's head as Rita poked her head in round the door.

"I hope you're going to be picking that up." She scolded playfully. Rita was their line manager and was the loveliest person Bonnie had ever met.

"Bonnie, come with me for a second, would you?"

Exchanging a look with George, who mouthed *'You're in trouble.'* Bonnie rose from her chair and followed Rita out into the hallway. She didn't stop there, however, instead leading Bonnie out into the stairwell.

"What's wrong?" She asked as Rita peered over the stair rail to see whether anyone was on the stairs or any of the lower levels. It was highly doubtful; the stairs only really got used when the elevators were broken, or when someone wanted to make a personal phone call and not get caught.

"You'll never guess what I heard last night on my way out." Rita grinned. She was a terrible gossip, but sometimes it had its advantages.

"What?"

"I heard management upstairs talking about a certain someone getting a promotion!"

"Really, who?"

"Oh, just a certain someone that might be going on holiday tomorrow." Bonnie gawked at Rita; she couldn't be talking about her! It wasn't possible. She'd already been passed over for promotion several times in the past, why would they choose to promote her now?

"Are you sure?" She clapped her hand to her mouth and Rita nodded, laughing as Bonnie jumped up and down on the spot and squealed.

"Really?" She asked, "You're not winding me up or anything?"

"Bonnie, have I ever lied to you?"

"I'm sorry, I didn't mean..."

"It's alright, I know what you meant." Rita smiled, pushing a hand through her red-brown hair, "Now we'd better get back to work. And remember, you can't breathe a word of this to anyone. They're going to offer you the promotion when you get back."

"I won't."

"And remember to act surprised."

The rest of the day passed in a blur of happiness and mind-numbing data entry. When they had gone back to the office, George had wanted to know what Bonnie had been told off about and Bonnie had happily replied that it was just girl talk. When he pressed further, she'd had to tell him that Rita had asked her to pick up some sanitary towels on her break. That did it. After that, he didn't want to know. Boys were squeamish about the stupidest things.

Gathering her things together, Bonnie shut down her PC and headed to the ladies' room. The toilets on trains were always filthy, not to mention the fact that they smelt terrible. She always went to the bathroom before leaving work so that she wouldn't need it on the way home.

"What did you need to talk to me about so desperately?" Inside a cubicle, Bonnie heard two people enter the bathroom.

"I have some news that you are not going to believe." A second voice replied, Bonnie thought she recognised them, but the building she worked in was huge, and it could be any number of people.

137

"Have you been listening to Rita again? You know she's full of crap, right?"

"Whatever, when you hear this you're going to laugh."

The girls' conversation was broken up here, by the sound of someone else flushing the toilet, and Bonnie had to strain to try and hear over it, curious about this latest piece of gossip.

"You mean that black lesbian on fourth floor?"

"That's the one."

"Why's she getting promoted and not you?" Bonnie almost choked at this; surely they couldn't be talking about her promotion? There had to be someone else. Yes, she worked on fourth floor, but she wasn't a lesbian.

"Rumour has it that management needs to balance the books if you know what I mean..."

"Er, no. Not really."

Bonnie heard a clucking sound and assumed that the gossip had clicked her tongue at her friend's stupidity.

"They're promoting her to show that they're into diversity..."

Bonnie had heard enough. She knew exactly what the gossip meant and didn't want to spend a second longer listening to her vile voice. Flushing the toilet, Bonnie gathered her things and exited the cubicle as noisily as she could. The look of horror on their faces did nothing to dispel the sick feeling Bonnie felt in the pit of her stomach, not even as the women blanched and quickly took one of the empty cubicles each.

Bonnie washed her hands, dried them and left hoping she'd managed to look a hell of a lot calmer than she felt. As she waited at the station for the train home, she decided that she would go out tonight. Either with friends or by herself, she didn't care at this point. Just as long as she could forget for a while.

Graham Ahern

Graham was in his room hiding from his parents. He'd been avoiding his mother ever since he'd run into her outside the Dr Wainright's office. They were going to have questions that he wasn't ready to answer yet.

"Graham!" He heard his dad yell up the stairs, "Get down here!" Well there went his genius plan of pretending he wasn't home. Shit. If he didn't go down, they'd only come up to him and then he'd be cornered. Heart sinking, Graham drudged out of his room and went to find his parents. They were waiting for him in the kitchen. Both of them were drinking. He took a seat on the opposite side of the small dining table and waited.

"I ssssaw you today." His mum slurred, pointing at him with a beer bottle.

"I know mum."

"And you ran away. You ran away from your own mother."

"I'm sorry, mum."

"What did I do to deserve you?" She spat, and Graham flinched. He was definitely going to take Dr. Wainright's advice and ask if he could move in with his Aunt. Weeping, his mum turned to the side and buried her face in her husband's shoulder dramatically. He lifted an arm around her and glared at Graham.

"What were you doing there?" He asked.

"I was seeing my psychiatrist." Graham admitted.

"You ain't got a psychiatrissst." His dad was slurring his words, too. Great.

"Yes I do. Her name is Dr. Wainright."

"Liar!" His mother yelled, resurfacing from his dad's shoulder suddenly. "You've been telling child services on me, I know it. You're the reason I had that visitor last week."

"It weren't me mum, I swear, it was probably that Mrs. Donnelly down the road. You know she don't like you." Graham started to panic. His parents were in a right state, and it never ended well.

"Aren't we good enough for you?" His dad demanded, slamming his fist on the table. Graham held his tongue, afraid of what might come out if he spoke. "Would you rather go live with someone else?"

When Graham didn't answer, his dad started to turn red in the face. "You will answer me when I'm talking to you, boy." He roared, rising from the table and pulling back his arm. Graham's eyes widened in fear. There was only one way this was going to end if he didn't move. He pushed back from the table and ran from the room, his parents didn't follow, they just sat called abuse from the kitchen.

As he fled the house, the last words he heard were; "Don't come back, you queer!" It was raining outside, and without a coat or anything to shelter him from it, he was going to get soaked. He decided to go to his Aunts for the night. She'd take care of him. Thankfully, she didn't live far away. He ran away from his house, hands clenching and unclenching as he fought the need to hit something, anything. Just to take his mind off things. The noise of his feet splashing against the pavement wasn't enough.

Dark thoughts crossed his mind. Thoughts he'd had many times in the past. Maybe he should just kill himself. He'd heard the same from his parents often enough. On a night like this it was harder to dampen the thoughts. Out of the corner of his eye, Graham saw movement. Turning to look, he saw the black kid that lived down the street. They were the same age. Maybe in a different world they could have been friends.

Right now, though, he didn't need a friend he needed a distraction. Clenching his fists again, he turned and headed towards him.

Ethan Foy

Ethan had been at the camp for a few days now, but he'd been so busy with activities that he hadn't even had a chance to track down the camp roster yet. He'd made it in time for the induction, just barely, but before he could find out anyone else's names they'd been split off into boy and girl groups for a quick tour of the cabins to find out which one they'd been assigned to Lead.

The rest of that day had been so hectic that Ethan had barely any time to remember his own name, let alone anyone else's. Today, however, he was going to change that. He had the whole afternoon off. A rare achievement, but it meant he could look for Helen.

"Knock knock." Ethan grinned, poking his head around the door to Cabin One, which was basically Camp HQ.

"I don't have time to deal with you today," July Winters bristled as she saw Ethan in the doorway.

"And a good afternoon to you too, July." Ethan grinned, leaning against the door frame of the cabin with his arms crossed.

"What do you want, Ethan?"

"I just came to see you."

"What do you really want?"

"I'm insulted that you would think so low of me!" Ethan brought a hand to his chest and pretended to be so hurt.

"I just know you." July replied with a smirk. "So, come on, dish. What is it you're after now?"

Ethan moved away from the door frame now and sat on the edge of her desk. "Okay, so maybe there is something I need you to do for me..."

"I knew it." July put down the papers she had been sorting through and turned to look at him. "So, what is it this time?"

"I need to take a peek at the camp roster. I'm looking for someone."

"A special someone?"

"Why, would you be jealous?"

"Of you? Please." July rolled her eyes although Ethan knew from past experience that she liked him. It seemed that since last camp, July had learnt her lesson and wasn't going to help him out just because he came in and batted his eyes at her.

"So, what's it gonna take for me to get a look at that roster?" Ethan narrowed his eyes. July leant back in her chair and clasped her hands beneath her chin like an evil villain as she thought about it. Ethan could practically see the cogs turning as she went over her list of disgusting things she could get him to clean. Or the boring activities she could get him to organise. This Helen chick better be worth it.

July sighed, "Fine, I'll let you look at the camp roster..."

"What's the catch?"

July grinned up at him like a Cheshire cat. "I want you to be my date to the end of camp dance."

"That's all?"

"Yup."

"You're not going to ask me to do your dish duty for the rest of the week, or watch the eleven-year olds tie knots or anything like that?"

"Nope. Just a date to the dance."

"Well, I think that can definitely be arranged." Ethan beamed. "Can I see the roster now?"

"I suppose." She sighed, opening one of the draws on the desk and pulling out a folder. Rifling through it and making sure that Ethan couldn't peek into it, she drew out a couple of sheets of paper and handed them to him.

He took them gladly and leafed through it. It was in alphabetical order, but since he had no idea what Helen's surname was, it didn't help at all. After reading through a page and a half, however, he realised that the lists had been split into boys and girls. Throwing down the two boys pages he had read through, and then a couple more, he started to look through the pages of girl's names.

Altogether, there were two Helens attending camp as a Leader this year. He didn't know either of them, so he couldn't narrow it down any further than that. Making a mental note of the two names, he handed July the roster.

"Thanks." He smiled.

"Find your special someone?" She smiled acidly.

"Come on July, you know you're my special someone!" Ethan teased, "But yes, I found the name I was looking for. Now I just need to find her."

"Her?"

Ethan nodded and grinned, watching the look on July's face. There was jealousy in there that was for sure.

"She's an ex from school." Ethan lied. "I heard she was coming to camp this year, so I thought I'd look her up. You know, say hi and what not." He wiggled his eyebrows and as July shot him a look that could melt glass, he decided to make a quick exit. After all, he had a girl to find.

Now that he had names and cabin numbers, he knew exactly where to go. Not to the cabins, but to the chores list in the main hall where he could find out which chores each of the Helen's cabins would currently be doing. As luck would have it, Cabin Six A had been paired with his own cabin; Seven B and Six A was led by one of the Helens. Because he'd scored the afternoon off, however, he could've missed out on meeting her altogether. If he'd just taken his chores instead of trading off with someone, he wouldn't have had to make the stupid deal with July, or wasted the last couple hours playing detective.

Upon entering the canteen, Ethan had an idea. Instead of working his way around the room and asking his friends if they knew who the Helens were and then trying to drop Soul Echo in to a conversation, he could save himself a lot of trouble.

The main part of the canteen was quiet, with only a few people were out there mopping the floor. That meant that almost everybody else on this chore shift would be in the back. It was a lot louder in the back, lots of chatter from the various conversations mingling with the clattering of plates being stacked, pots being hung and cutlery being put in drawers. Climbing up on to a table and placing two fingers in his mouth, Ethan whistled as loud as he could. It worked! Everyone stopped what they were doing and turned to face him.

Farrell Brennan

Farrell's heart was pounding in his ears, his chest was burning, and he could barely breathe, but he just wanted to get home. He'd gone out to try and avoid his parents. They were still expecting him to flip out about this whole adoption thing, and when his mother saw the black eye he'd just got, she'd try and say that he was finally acting out.

Slipping in quietly through the front door, Farrell went straight up the stairs and into the bathroom where he leant on the sink and looked at himself in the mirror; that jerk down the street, Grant, he thought his name was, had gotten him good and proper this time. Not only was his eye throbbing, but his ribs ached, and he was sure that if he lifted his top he'd see a mosaic of bruises covering him. He couldn't face looking right at them now though, and honestly, he wasn't sure whether he'd be able to lift his arms that high.

Although he knew that he wasn't going to be able to get away with hiding his face from his parents forever, Farrell retreated to his bedroom and the only sanctuary he really had; the internet. Sure, there were bullies there too, but at least he didn't have to try and outrun them. All he had to do was block them, or just switch to a different chat room. On the internet, hateful messages could just be deleted.

Opening a web browser, he headed to the Soul Echo site. Ever since finding out that the others like him were interacting there, he'd been lurking. He'd posted an introduction like everyone else, but other than that there wasn't much going on. Maybe everyone was too shy, or not used to forums that they weren't sure exactly what they could and couldn't do.

Today there was a new thread and Farrell clicked to open it. This one was a photo thread, and it had been started by Cam. He opened it, curious to put a face to the usernames. Cam was a beautiful blond with expressive blue eyes. She dressed well, and it looked like she exercised to keep in shape. Unfortunately, she looked like one of those girls that knew she was pretty and was very proud of it. Farrell would put money on her being able to twist her father around her little finger.

Judging by the times on the posts, no-one else had been brave enough to submit their own photographs for the next twenty-four hours. It had been Aaron that had been brave enough to post a photo next. He was tall from the looks of it, and a medium build. He had dark hair brushed neatly and dark green eyes. He wasn't sure, but Farrell thought he could see a crucifix in the background; perhaps Aaron or his family were religious, then.

The next picture sent Farrell scooting backwards in his chair trying to get as far away from the computer screen as possible. A cold chill washed over him and his heart sank to the pit of his stomach. This had to be some sort of horrible joke. A really elaborate one set out to humiliate and torture him. Right? Taking a deep breath, he moved back to the computer and read the post.

It wasn't a joke. This was real. And it proved that the world really was a small and horrible place. The third picture was of Graham Ahern. Farrell's tormentor. His name wasn't Grant as he'd thought, after all. To think that they had something so unique in common made Farrell want to throw up, and he instantly felt sorry for whichever one of these poor girls had been paired with such a monster. After the shock of seeing Graham's face, Farrell couldn't bear to look at the rest of the thread, let alone post one of his own right now, so he shut down his computer, turned on his stereo and lay back on his bed.

How could Graham be so different online compared to real life? On the forum (his user name was Cyclone), Graham came across as a genuinely nice person. He'd even participated in conversations in the introductions thread.

147

Should he go back and post a picture, or would he just be giving Graham more fire to throw at him? There was a great atmosphere on the forum at the moment, and Farrell felt accepted for the first time in a long while. No. If he kept quiet it would be better for everyone. Part of him was angry that Graham had managed to invade another part of his life and he was angry at himself for being intimidated enough to not out the bullying git to the other eight. What if they took Graham's side? Or he started to bully the others, too?

Imogen Chidwick

Imogen had looked everywhere, but she couldn't for the life of her find that bloody letter. It wasn't in her desk drawers. It wasn't under the keyboard on her computer. It wasn't even in the pile of papers that sat next to her bed. She just couldn't find it. She'd been looking for it for so long that she couldn't even remember why she had wanted it in the first place. Maybe to look it up on the internet or something.

Giving up, she made herself a coffee and decided to spend the afternoon curled up with a good book. She was reading a couple at the moment, and could do with finishing one or two of them off before she started anymore.

Sinking into a chair, she pulled her book towards her and opened it. There, marking her place, was the letter that she'd just spent ages looking for. Cursing her own stupidity, she found a scrap of paper to replace it, and took the letter to the computer.

She went to the HSSE website and had a read. It all seemed pretty straight forward. When she went back to the main page, and found a link to something called Soul Echo. Curiosity got the better of her and she was pleasantly surprised when she found that it led to a forum dedicated to the ten of them.

Books forgotten, Imogen settled into her computer chair and started to read through the forum, intrigued with the idea of getting to know these others like her.

Dr. David Cole

David cracked his knuckles, agitated. The experiment was going well, albeit slowly. He'd tried to petition early activation of the implants, but Hunter had disagreed as usual and unfortunately his word was final. Had he been a younger, more foolish man, David probably would have started the activation early anyway but throwing it all away over some pissing contest with Hunter would be ridiculous. He'd have to think of some other way to get back at the damned idiot.

There was a knock at the door and he sighed audibly, reaching up to loosen his tie.

"Go away!" He yelled, not in the mood to see anyone unless they were here to say that Hunter had changed his mind. The door opened anyway, and he looked up from his desk to see who it was.

"Well, speak of the devil and he shall appear." David scowled as the very man he had just been cursing stepped into his office.

"Good afternoon, David." Hunter smiled.

"What do you want?" David demanded, rising to his feet. "Come to apologise?"

"Actually no."

"Then get out." David turned his back on the younger man and stalked over to check the various monitors that were blinking away in the corner of his office. They held the vital signs of their ten subjects, it was less detailed than the system he had in the lab, but he liked to be able to monitor them whenever and wherever he pleased.

"I came to discuss your rather, uh, heated discussions with Dr. Ranford."

"What's it got to do with you?" David asked without bothering to turn around.

"I think it would be better for everyone if you could refrain from having your arguments in the corridors."

"Would you rather I scheduled a meeting room?" David asked, turning to face Hunter finally, "You've got everything else on a schedule. How's Tuesdays at eleven? I think I have those free. I'll let Linden know, shall I? Get her to pencil me in."

Hunter sighed. "You know that's not what I meant. Why do you have to be so bloody defensive all the time?"

"Well maybe if you weren't such an idiot, things would run better around here."

"If I'm the idiot, why am I the one in charge?"

David was very close to seeing red. Hunter loved to rub it in that he was the lead scientist, a right that should have been David's many, many years ago.

"I don't know!" He fumed. Hunter had picked the wrong time to come and start this conversation, and David was going to let him have it. "Why did daddy's little boy get lead scientist when daddy died? What a mystery. I don't know how we'll ever solve this one." Feeling more than a little smug, David settled back down at his desk as Hunter stomped out his office without bothering to reply. He probably needed time to come up with a witty retort. He loved winding him up, it was so damned easy.

Ethan Foy

"I have a message for Helen. You have a phone call from someone at Soul Echo. Please report to the Cabin One at once. Thanks." Ethan jumped down from the table he'd climbed up on and exited the room, waiting outside to ambush Helen as she came out. It didn't take long.

"Oh god, you scared me!" She cried, flinching away from him.

He looked at her for a moment. She was quite pretty, but not in the obvious way. She had long brown hair pulled back into a high pony tail. Deep chestnut eyes, and plump lips. Her body wasn't half bad either, but then it was a sports camp. Most of the people here were in shape.

"I'm sorry, I didn't mean to." He apologised.

"Hey wait!" He called as she started to walk away from him.

"I have a phone call to get to, remember?" She called back, raising an eye brow at him.

"Yeah, about that. I lied."

Helen stopped and turned to face him, hands on her hips. "You did what?"

"Didn't you think it was weird that someone from Soul Echo would be calling you? Have you even given any of them the phone number for this place?"

"Well, yeah, but I-Wait a minute. How do you know about Soul Echo?"

Ethan smiled and held out his hand. "Allow me to introduce myself. I'm Ethan Foy. Number five. You must be Helen, Number eight."

"You're part of the experiment, too?" Helen asked, her eyes widening in realisation. Ethan nodded. "How did you know I was here?"

"I checked the forum just before I left home to come here, and I saw your post."

"But how did you find me? I didn't exactly spell out exactly where I was going. I didn't even leave my surname!"

"I have friends in high places here. I took a chance and checked the camp roster; you know, just in case you really were coming here. As for the surname thing, that's why I made up the phone call thing. I knew there were two Helens, and you would both be there, it was just a process of elimination."

Helen removed a hand from her hip and brought it to eye level where she rubbed at her temples for a little bit.

"I can't believe this is happening." She sighed.

"I know, isn't is awesome?" Ethan grinned.

"Hardly. I thought that coming to camp this year would let me get away from this whole experiment thing for a while."

"Things been rough at home?"

"Kind of. I mean, I always knew I was adopted, but the whole experiment thing is just weird. How can you expect that?"

"You knew you were adopted? I thought our parents weren't allowed to tell us anything."

"My parents didn't tell me. I found the adoption papers when I was little."

"Oh."

"Well, I guess I'm going to go back inside now." Helen said after a long silence.

"What, why?"

"I just... I can't deal with this right now. I'm sorry Ethan."

"I understand. If you want to chat about this or anything though, just come and find me. I'm in cabin Seven B."

"Yeah, ok, I guess I'll see you around then." Helen smiled before turning and going back into the Canteen. Ethan followed half way and sat on the steps outside. He was a little disappointed about how it had gone, but it was to be expected. Not everyone was going to take it the same. And she had said that she had come to camp to get away from everything.

Ah well. Maybe when she'd had a few days to think about it, she'd track him down. It'd be nice to know someone else in the same situation. They were busy, however, and Ethan wasn't sure whether they'd get the chance to talk to each other again. With the end of camp coming up, all the Camp Leaders had to prepare everything to be cleaned down and packed away ready to go into storage until next year.

Jennifer Dillon

Jen paced back and forth anxiously in the living room. Her parents were on their way back from the airport and would be home any minute. Thankfully her sisters had both gone out with the twins and they wouldn't be back till late. It was the perfect time to ask her parents about the letter.

She'd waited the whole time they had been away, considering phoning them and demanding to know what it was all about, and she almost did several times. Instead patience won out, and she'd spent some time checking out the forum - Soul Echo - and getting to know the others like her. Their parents had all kept it from them, too, but they had all known about it for days by the time Jen had found the forum.

Had her parents really been planning to keep everything from her? Through some of the others, she'd discovered that their parents had been contractually bound to tell each of them when the letters had arrived, that they had all agreed to it when they'd adopted them.

Hearing a car pull into the drive, Jen's first reaction was to storm outside and have it out with them on the driveway, but did she really want to broadcast it to the entire street? Probably not. She also considered going out to help her parents unload the car but decided against it figuring she wouldn't be able to hold her tongue long enough.

No, she was going to sit on the sofa and pretend to watch TV while she waited for them to finish bringing everything in. An absolutely agonising twenty minutes later, her parents finally sauntered into the living room. The two of them actually looked very happy and Jen felt a little bad about having to ruin their good moods, but this was more important.

"Hey sweetheart." Her mother trilled. "What's that you've got there?" She gestured for the letter in Jen's hand.

"Just a letter about my implant." She replied. Her mother blanched, which was quite a feat considering how red she was from her time in the sun.

"Where did you find that?" She demanded, trying to snatch it away but Jen was faster and moved out of her reach. "You had no right to go through my things!" She looked up at Jen's father for back up.

"Give us the letter, Jennifer." He said, his voice stern and steady. "Give us the letter and let's forget this whole thing never happened." Right, like that was going to happen.

"No! I want to know why you weren't going to tell me about this!"

"We didn't want you to feel like you were some kind of freak." Her mother told her, "Or that you weren't part of the family anymore."

"Or maybe you were too embarrassed to admit that your daughter is part of a science experiment?" Jen asked, crossing her arms.

"No of course not!"

"So, what is it?"

"We just want you to lead a normal life!"

"A life of lies isn't normal!"

Jen's father stepped forwards and plucked the letter from her hand. She didn't protest, knowing she had a picture of the letter on her phone.

"Right, let's talk about this." He frowned. "And then we'll have nothing more to do with it."

Bonnie Kinsella

Bonnie woke up feeling rough. She had had a lot to drink last night and couldn't remember anything that had happened after around ten pm. Rubbing her eyes, she tried to sit up and realised she couldn't, there was a weight over her shoulder. Looking around her, she realised that she was in someone else's bed!

Had she been so drunk the night before that she had agreed to go home with someone? This was bad. Very bad. Slowly and carefully, Bonnie wriggled out from under the mystery man's arm, got dressed and slipped out of his house. Luckily, she recognised the area and it wasn't too long before she was in a taxi on her way home.

Once home, she made some coffee and went to her computer intending to do some of the work she had brought home for the weekend. Yet she couldn't concentrate on it. Instead, she decided to check out Soul Echo. She had taken to visiting the Soul Echo website almost obsessively to see if anything new was going on. Clicking on to it now, she had an idea; what if the ten of them met up! It would be great. They had been talking to each other for weeks now, so a little meet up should naturally be the next step to take.

She clicked the button for a new topic and quickly typed in her idea, hoping that everyone else would be as receptive to it.

We should meet.

Posted by **KinnyBee**.

I'm bored. Sooooo I was thinking, we all know each other well enough by now, right? I think it's time for us to meet. Somewhere like

London might be the easiest place? Unless we all live in the same sort of area?

Hopefully some of you guys will agree. It doesn't have to be anything huge. Just a simple day out for anyone who wants to come. Please reply to this and let me know if anyone is interested! We can sort out a plan of action and a date after that.

Oh. And I think we should have something to identify each other by - you know like how people go on blind dates and they hold a rose or something. I think we should do something similar, but it can't be too wacky or hard to get hold of. I was thinking we could use something blue. Like a scarf?

Any ideas?

Bonnie.

Bonnie read over her post a few times before deciding it was ok and hitting post. Hopefully everyone else would be online soon and she would get an answer. As it turned out, she didn't have to wait long at all. Within half an hour she got a notification letting her know that someone had responded to her post. She clicked it eagerly, finding not one answer, but many.

RE: We should meet.

Posted by **Candi.**

I think this is a great idea! London is easy for me to get too, so that's fine. I'm not so sure on the blue, but I guess I can make an exception for you guys.
What about this weekend? If that's alright with everyone's schedules.

How long will we be staying, and will there be drinking? Just wondering whether it would be a good idea for us to find a hotel or something.

RE: We should meet.

Posted by **Immo.**

I'm for a meet if you guys are. I can't wait!

I have something blue I can wear.

Staying over in a hotel would be a lot easier for me, otherwise I'd have to leave pretty early to make the last bus back to my house. As long as it's somewhere cheap though. I can't afford anything over the top!

What about a youth hostel? I bet we could book a room in one of those for cheaps.

RE: We should meet.

Posted by **Candi.**

Ew! Youth hostels are seriously gross. There is no way I'm staying in one of those; they're communal for crying out loud! I'm fine with staying in a relatively cheap hotel, but there is no way I could stay in a youth hostel.

What about the Ramada Grand?

RE: We should Meet.

Posted by **D0M1N1C.**

The Ramada Grand isn't cheap! Not by any stretch of the imagination! I'll do some research and find some that are less than fifty quid a night. That should do everyone, right? Maybe I could look into bed and breakfasts as well.

A meet up sounds great, though.

RE: We should meet.

Posted by **Immo.**

I'm not sure you will find a bed and breakfast in London for under fifty quid a night! My grandparents run one over in Camden and they take in at least sixty-five pounds per person per night. And they're one of the cheaper ones! A

hotel is probably our best bet. If we do a group
booking we can probably get a discount.

RE: We should Meet.

Posted by **D0M1N1C.**

Okay, good idea! I'll send a few emails out
once I've found the cheapest ones then. Forgot to
add before, but this weekend would be fine for
me.

RE: We should meet.

Posted by **Immo.**

Me too. This weekend I mean.

This is brilliant! Bonnie thought to herself. The meet up idea
was going down a treat, and from the looks of things, she would be able
to sit back and let it organise itself while taking all of the credit. Pushing
away from the computer, she wandered over to her wardrobe to try
and decide what to wear for this meet up. After pushing coat hangers
back and forth for a while, Bonnie clicked her tongue and sighed.
Nothing in there would do. This called for some shopping.

Pushing the wardrobe doors closed with a grin, she plucked her
coat and handbag from the back of her bedroom door and skipped out
of her room.

Farrell Brennan

Loading up the Soul Echo forum, Farrell was surprised to find a meet up thread. He'd been expecting it to happen sooner or later, but he had always thought it would be later. The prospect of meeting the others excited and terrified him at the same time. What if Graham decided he was going to go as well? He wasn't sure if he wanted Graham to know about him – Farrell still hadn't posted in the picture thread yet because he was worried about the repercussions.

Full of trepidation, he checked the thread to see who'd posted to say they wanted to go, but relief soon flooded his body when he found that Graham's name wasn't there. Either he hadn't posted because he wasn't interested, or he just hadn't seen the thread yet. Either way, Farrell hoped Graham's name would stay off the list.

He posted a quick message himself saying that he was interested and laughing when he saw the suggestion that everyone wore a single blue glove. They were going to look like idiots. Talk in the thread had quickly turned to attractions in London and the consensus so far seemed to be the aquarium because it was indoors and would probably be quieter so they could talk. Farrell had never been to the Aquarium, so he was excited to go.

A weekend away from his family would be pure bliss and Farrell found himself looking forward to something for the first time in a long time. But then he realised he'd was going to have to tell them that he was going. Great. Either they were going to love that he was meeting with the others and encourage him to go or they were going to worry that he was running away from them and make him feel guilty. He wasn't sure which was worse. Getting up from the PC, Farrell went downstairs to talk to his parents.

Dr. Linden Ranford

Linden sat at her desk tapping a well-manicured fingernail against her coffee cup. It was official, she was bored. There'd been no new developments for hours now, and she was bored of obsessively refreshing the Soul Echo forum; a responsibility she'd quickly handed over to Juniper to keep her fidgety assistant out of her office for a while.

She had been excited when Dr. Hunter had first told them that the subjects had set up an internet forum to get to know each other on, and even handed him the password so that they too could log in and see what was going on. With the only condition being that they were to observe only. No contact.

The subjects, as it turned out, were far less outgoing than Linden had imagined. It took over a week before they'd even posted pictures of each other. Pictures that had then been printed out and pinned to the wall in the main lab. It was great to finally have faces to go with the names and numbers that adorned the wall. Of course, they had had the baby pictures up, but it was fascinating to see how they'd changed in the past seventeen years.

It had nagged at her the whole time that she couldn't see how they were progressing through the years. One of the main points in any experiment was observation. Watching to see what happens, seeing the outcome and understanding how they got to that point.

With this experiment, they had seen the beginning; from production of the implant to the search for the babies, to the implantation phase and then that was pretty much it. The only thing they could monitor right now were the readings being transmitted from

163

the implants that let them know their subjects were still alive and that the implants themselves were working just fine.

As her stomach growled, Linden remembered why she had been sitting at her desk just doing nothing; she had been waiting for the canteen to open. She almost never ate in there, preferring instead to bring her own lunch, but today she had forgotten it. It rankled, knowing that her chicken salad was sat on the stairs just going to waste.

Taking her coffee cup with her, she rose from her seat. The canteen would be open now, and she could sate her hunger for a while. Her hand was barely around the door handle, however, when it opened and she was damn near ploughed down by a mass of frizzy hair and lab coat.

"Juniper!" She cried out, almost tearing her own lab coat off as her coffee exploded down the front of it. Luckily, the white silk shirt she was wearing underneath had avoided the same brown stained fate as the coat.

"Ah!" Juniper cried as she stumbled into the room and managed to catch herself on the chairs opposite Linden's desk before she hit the floor.

"So, to what do I owe this pleasure?" Linden asked dryly, carefully hanging her soiled lab coat on the hook on the back of her door. Juniper looked at her, confused.

"You barged into my office without knocking, I assume you have something you desperately need to tell me." She prompted.

Juniper seemed to come back to her senses. "Oh! Yes." Linden saw her eyes flick to the lab coat. "I am sorry, I'll take that to be cleaned when I am done."

"The reason..."

"Yes, of course. I came in here to tell you that they've scheduled a meet up!" Juniper explained, almost jumping for joy at the end of the sentence.

Instantly knowing who they were, Linden returned to her desk and went straight to the Soul Echo forum. Out of the corner of her eye, she noticed that her assistant had taken a seat opposite her and was waiting patiently for Linden to react.

According to the forum, they were indeed planning a meet up. And soon.

"Well, it seems we have a lot to prepare." Linden smiled, leaning back in her chair.

"We're going too?" Juniper asked. She caught on quick, it was one of the things Linden liked about her.

"Of course. This is a perfect research opportunity, there is no way I could pass this up."

"Do you think Dr. Hunter will allow it?"

"He better. Although if he says no, we'll just go anyway." Linden sneered. Dr. Hunter would probably just let her go if she kicked up enough of a stink. There would be conditions of course, she could imagine him lecturing her now: "do not talk to them, do not draw attention to yourselves, do not interfere with what they are doing under any circumstances." Blah blah blah. He was a stickler for rules and restrictions.

"So, what's first on the agenda?" Juniper asked, pulling a notepad and pen out of the pocket on her lab coat to make a list.

"Well for starters you can make me a fresh coffee and fetch me a clean lab coat." She laughed inwardly as Juniper scribbled these things down before realising that Linden was teasing her again. Making a noise a bit like a humph, Juniper rose from her chair, grabbed Linden's coffee cup and stalked from the room.

Dammit. She watched the door close, thinking that she should have asked Juniper to bring her back something to eat as well. Picking up the pager on her desk, she realised that she still could and sent her a message with a wicked smile.

So far it seemed as though the meeting was going to happen in London. That would be perfect; there are more than enough people milling around London every day for them to follow them around and not stand out or look suspicious. As soon as Juniper got back with lunch and coffee they could make a plan for the day.

Dr. Juniper Renwells

As she hurried from Linden's office, Juniper muttered under her breath, scolding herself for being such an idiot. She had been hoping to get back into Linden's good books with the latest news from the forum, but that had gone right out the window. That's what you got for being impatient. It was the bane of her life sometimes.

Realising she was swinging Linden's favourite mug back and forth as she walked, Juniper brought it to her chest and cradled it carefully; it would be just her luck to accidentally smash it against the wall or something. That was just what her day needed.

The news of the meet up seemed to have gone down well. It was a major development, a chance for them to get out there and do some actual observations, not just theoretical ones. The two of them would finally be able to answer some of the questions that had been piling up over the years; had any of them reacted oddly to the chip, had they all gone through puberty etc. Opening the door to the break room and setting the mug by the kettle which she flicked on, Juniper jumped and suppressed a squeal as her phone vibrated in her pocket.

Quickly pulling it out to see what was wrong, she frowned down at her screen. It was Linden. Of course it was Linden. She wanted Juniper to take her some food back with the coffee. No please or thank you.

She waited there patiently for the kettle to boil before realising it would probably be a lot easier if she went to the canteen first. If she took the coffee there and back with her she'd probably end up spilling most of it. It didn't take her long to grab what Linden wanted, as well as something for herself before going back to finish the coffee.

Knocking politely on Linden's office door, Juniper waited to be called in. After the near miss earlier she wasn't going to take any more chances. If she screwed up again, Linden would probably ban her from going to London with her. When there was no response, Juniper tried the handle. The office was locked. Her phone buzzed in her pocket again and she carefully moved her phone to her other hand to check the message.

Meet me in Conference room 21. L.

Cursing lightly, Juniper slid her phone away and turned away Linden's office, her crisp-laden lab coat pockets rustling as she moved. At least she could to take the lift up to the conference room.

Dr. David Cole

David was having a hard time believing what he was hearing. He'd just found out that the subjects were coordinating a meet up, and that Hunter not only knew but was doing absolutely nothing to monopolise on this opportunity! He himself had little interest in the Soul Echo website that had been set up by one of the subjects and wanted no part of it, preferring instead to deal with the figures and read-outs they received from the implants. If Linden hadn't brought forward the idea of going to London and observing them he would have been none the wiser.

That was one of the many reasons that he preferred Linden over Hunter, she simply had the analytical mind that suited this field of work. She was curious, studious and thorough. Her being easy on the eyes was a big plus, too, since most female scientists were either old crones or batty young things like Linden's assistant Renwells.

Speaking of whom, David looked up just in time to see her bustle through the conference room door, her pockets laden with food and a coffee in her hand.

"Ah, at last!" Linden smiled, rising from her chair to retrieve her food, and the coffee before her assistant had chance to drop it. She'd already destroyed a lab coat today, from the sounds of it.

"I hope you bought enough food for all of us." David raised an eyebrow, addressing Linden rather than her assistant. He watched with vindictive pleasure as Renwells started to empty her pockets of food. She'd clearly bought some of it for herself to eat, and wasn't sure whether she'd have to give it up.

169

"Don't worry about me, I have already eaten." Hunter called across the table without looking up from his laptop.

"Is chicken salad alright for you Dr. Cole?" Renwells asked him politely, offering him her lunch.

"Perfect. Thank you ever so much." He smiled, though he could feel Linden's glare burning into the side of his head. She hated it when he tormented her assistant. Renwells took her place by Linden's side like an obedient dog beside its master and opened a packet of crisps.

"So." David announced when he'd finished eating, breaking the silence, "Are you going to explain to us why you were going to keep this meet up to yourself?"

"I didn't realise that I had to run absolutely everything by you, I told you about the forum so that we could all keep track, and to avoid situations like this." Dr. Hunter replied, finally closing his laptop.

"And I told you at that time that I had no intention of fawning over some stupid website, so you would have to keep me informed either way."

"Well, now you do know, so what's the problem?"

"The problem, is that we have an invaluable opportunity here. To observe them without the restraints of being in a laboratory; something we never had the chance to do with Adam or Eve. This is a chance to test aspects of the implant that we would otherwise only be able to theorise about! Now's our chance to prove that they are actually working! And you're saying no?"

"That is exactly what I am saying."

David found himself rising from his seat now, getting irritated with that idiot Hunter. He had never cared about this experiment the way David would, so why on earth the position of Lead Scientist had been left to him would forever be a mystery. One that he hoped he could one day solve and rectify. Until then, he could only do his best to try and further improve the experiment. Even if it meant going against Hunter.

"So if neither I nor Linden had bothered to check the forum, you would have kept quiet about this whole thing. You would have let them meet up and just read about what they might have posted on the forum later on?"

"Yes."

"Your father would be ashamed of you-"

"You leave my father out of this!" Hunter cried, pushing back his own seat and standing too. The two of them stared at each other for a few moments before Linden quietly stood up and leant forwards with both her hands on the table.

"Look, if you two have finished this pissing contest then maybe we can talk about this like adults?"

David nodded, crossing his arms and focusing his attention on Linden instead. She held his gaze for a moment before turning towards Hunter.

"Right. We acknowledge that you are the lead scientist in this experiment." She paused and turned to David to make sure he nodded, "But you have also told us countless times that you view us as equals, and we should sort things out accordingly."

"Your point?" David asked, wondering where she was going with her little speech.

"I propose a vote. Majority rules. End of discussion. Are we agreed?" Both men narrowed their eyes but nodded their agreement.

"Okay. All those in favour of travelling to London to observe the subjects in person raise your hand."

David was pleased when she raised her hand along with him. Hunter scowled, obviously annoyed.

"And those opposed?"

Two hands shot into the air.

"Put your hand down, Juniper. You don't count." Linden turned to tell her assistant, who instantly withdrew her hand and looked down at her lap.

"So there we have it, majority rules in favour of observing the subjects in London. If you need me, I'll be in my office preparing for a field trip. Come on, Juniper." David watched, astounded, as Linden turned and swept out of the room with her assistant hot on her heels. Never had he been more impressed by a female scientist than he was right now.

"Was there anything else you wanted?" Hunter asked him, his face red as he scooped up his laptop.

"No, I'm quite satisfied for now." David smiled across the table at him, before gathering his things and resisting the urge to skip back to his office. He was finally going to get to test the implants, and there would be someone there to observe the effects! He'd waited so long for this!

Aaron Maysh

Aaron read through the meet up thread uncertainly. Did he want to meet up with the others? If he did there'd be no going back, no pretending that he was normal anymore. He'd be accepting that he was adopted, and that he was part of a science experiment.

Since receiving the letter and finding out that he'd been adopted, nothing more had been said on the matter. He knew that his parents would avoid the subject for as long as he wanted them to and though they tried to act normal, Aaron could see it there in their eyes. The way they looked at him now was different.

This revelation; this discovery, had changed them all. He tried to imagine how his parents must feel, they tried for eighteen years to keep their secret in the dark, and it was all revealed by a letter. They had condemned themselves to this lie when they had signed the contracts.

Maybe now that it was all out in the open, they felt a little better about it. A huge burden off their shoulders. One thing that Aaron knew for sure was that his mother had been praying more often than since the arrival of the letter. She had even started going to church every Sunday again, something she hadn't done since he and Jesse had been younger.

What would happen to his family if he went to this meet up? They were already a disjointed mess. Should he really risk tearing them further apart in order to pursue the very thing that had hurt them already? There was a knock at the door and Aaron shut the forum page quickly; a guilty feeling rushing over him as if he had just been caught sinning by a priest.

"Aaron, honey." His mother poked her head around the door, "Dinner's nearly ready."

"Alright mum, I'll be down in a minute."

Opening the web page again, he sighed. If he didn't go now, he'd regret it for the rest of his life.

Dr. Jeremy Hunter

Jeremy browsed through the Soul Echo forum. Since agreeing to place a link to it, he'd asked Number Four for access so that he could keep an eye on things; professional curiosity of course and today he kept wandering back to a thread Number Two had made about the ten of them meeting up.

He had mixed feelings about what had just happened in the meeting with David and Linden where they'd teamed up against him as usual. This time the two of them had voted on a trial activation of the implants while the ten were together in London. He had voted against it, it was far too early to be trying something like this, but the more he thought about it, the more he realised that they were right. This was a valuable opportunity. When was the next time that they could guarantee that one or more of the ten would be in the same place at the same time; within radar distance of each other so that their implants would react. And even if two of them did get together, nothing would happen unless they were paired.

Jeremy frowned at his computer screen and chewed on the end of his pencil. As much as he hated to admit it, David was right. Urgh, even thinking the words left a bad taste in his mouth. But he was. They had to activate the implants. For a moment he thought about going to the others and telling them that he had been wrong, but he knew that if he did he would never live it down.

No. He'd keep his approval secret for now. Who was he to upset the delicate balance of power? If he admitted his fault it would provide them with something to use against him if they ever tried to push him out of the company, and he wouldn't put something as low as that past them. It wasn't just paranoia either, he was sure of it. He could see it in their eyes and the way they treated him. Sometimes they just ignored him completely and acted as if they were in charge of the experiment.

A ping noise distracted him from his thoughts, and, looking down in shock Jeremy realised he'd snapped his pencil in half. Shaking his head with a sigh, he swept the pieces off his desk and into the bin. He definitely had to learn not to let the two of them bother him so much. He was starting to get grey hairs.

Aaron Maysh

Aaron looked at the empty chair beside him at the dining table. Of all the things that had changed since the letter, his brother's absence was the most painful. He and his brother Jesse had been close until now. Sometimes he wondered whether his parents wished that they could avoid him this easily. Did they envy Jesse?

Often, Aaron would see his mother looking forlornly at Jesse's empty chair Jesse. This was the time when the two of them would fill each other in on how their days had been. Of the two of them, Jesse had always been the closest to their mother and now Aaron knew why.

Jesse was the baby she'd been told by so many doctors that she'd never be able to carry. He was the baby that had survived against all odds. He wasn't the baby that had come from a laboratory. If anyone was to leave, it should be Aaron. He had no blood claim to the people that had raised him, to the brother that had abandoned him.

He thought about the others like him and wondered if they were experiencing the same kind of things. If he chose not to go to the meet up, he'd never know and it was oddly comforting to know that he wasn't the only one going through this. He thought about all of them a lot.

Bonnie seemed very lively, whereas Imogen was withdrawn. Ethan was athletic where he and Dominic were scrawny. Helen, like Ethan, was athletic where Graham seemed lazy. Camilla liked to shop, and Jennifer was saving to get her own place. He already felt like he knew them, just from their conversations online. Maybe he would like to meet them after all.

For all of their differences, they all had something in common. Something that tied them together. He wondered which of the girls possessed the implant paired with his own and thought about which of the others might have been paired also. Was it wrong of him to think he could guess just from their pictures online?

Aaron cleared his throat and put down his knife and fork. Here it goes. His stomach roiled like a stormy sea and he could feel himself sweating.

"Mum, dad." He waited for them both to look up at him. "I need to tell you something. I'm going to London this weekend, to see the other nine. The ones from the experiment. The ones like me."

"Now, Aaron, do you really think this is wise?" His father asked, and Aaron could see the disappointment in his eyes. He knew that his father had been hoping Aaron would just want to forget all about the experiment and have them go back to the way they were before.

"I've thought it through, and I think it's for the best." Aaron replied, trying to ignore the look of hurt he saw flash across his mother's face.

"Well," His father spoke, cutting short whatever protest his mother was about to voice, "If you think that this is something you have to do, then I'll support you."

Aaron looked at his father, shocked. "Really?" He'd been expecting an argument, tears, but not this.

"Of course. You are still my son. I will support you in anything you decide that you want to do. Within reason of course."

"Thanks, Dad." Aaron smiled gratefully, relieved. He looked at his mother who seemed to have lost her voice completely. Instead, she smiled and reached across the table to squeeze his hand with a nod. It was settled then, he was going to London.

Jennifer Dillon

Jen moved around her room quietly, pausing every time one of the floor boards creaked beneath her feet and waiting a few seconds to make sure she couldn't hear anyone else moving around the house. She felt a little bad about the stealth, but it was a necessary precaution.

When she'd confronted her parents about the letter from the laboratory, they'd told her everything she wanted to know. On one condition; that she forget about the whole thing and never asked them about it again.

She had agreed at the time, eager to hear everything her parents had to offer. It wasn't much. Just that they'd been thinking about adopting when this opportunity had come along. And now, her father reasoned, they had fulfilled their duties by telling Jen what she was part of. In his eyes, they didn't need to have anything more to do with it.

Her parents might not, but Jen needed to know more. There was no way she could go back to being plain old Jennifer Dillon, eldest daughter of Steve and Rachel Dillon. Not now that she had found an unexplored part of herself; this new Jennifer that was part of a group chosen to take part in an experiment that could change the world as they knew it.

This meet up with the others would be the first step in her new life and so for this reason, she was packing a bag in the middle of the night and trying to fabricate some sort of lie to throw her parents off where she was really going. Packing an overnight bag was hard going when one of her arms was in a sling still, but she was getting there.

Maybe she could get her grandmother to cover for her. She'd been very encouraging about the whole experience so far.

It was too late for Jen to call her now though, she'd have to get up early and try to get hold of her before her parents woke up. Once she was sure that she had everything, Jen tiptoed back across the room to her bed, set her alarm clock to wake her early the next morning and curled up beneath the duvet. She was so excited about going to London and meeting the others, however, that she lay staring at the ceiling for a long while until sleep finally claimed her.

Graham Ahern

It was finally the morning of the trip and Graham was, not for the first time, questioning whether or not he should go. He'd been changing his mind every day since he'd found out about it and he was sick of it, so he'd decided to go and see his psychiatrist one more time before he went.

The day before, when he'd been sure that he was definitely going, Graham had packed a bag to take to London. He slung it over his shoulder now as he left the house, not wanting to have to go back and get it if Dr. Wainright persuaded him to go.

As far as the others were concerned, he was still going. On one of the days where he was happy to be going, he had posted on the forum letting them all know. He'd regretted it the next day when his indecision kicked in but by then it was too late for him to change his mind. He didn't know how to delete the post he had made, and the others had already seen it and responded.

They'd all said that they were looking forward to meeting him, but his paranoia forbade him from believing it.

"How are you feeling today, Graham?" Dr. Wainright asked as he sat fidgeting on her sofa.

"Unsure." He replied, "Today's when I'm meant to be going to London."

"Aren't you going to?"

"I don't know. Do you think I should?"

181

Dr. Wainright put down her pen and reached up to take off her glasses. "Graham," She smiled. "I thought you had decided to go? You wanted to see that they were like you. That you're not alone."

"But what if they're not like me?"

"You'll never know unless you try, will you?" When Graham didn't reply, Dr. Wainright continued, "Meeting these others, the ones like you, it might give you some peace of mind about what's happened to you. Some of them might even have been through similar ordeals."

"So you mean they might be just as messed up as me?" Graham hadn't considered that. In his mind, the others had been these perfect unattainable people. A group that he could never fit in with, despite being one of them.

He hadn't been able to see far enough past his low self-esteem until now to even imagine that they all must have been adopted like him. That they'd all been given away by the people that were meant to love them the most. Their parents had abandoned them; had landed them in a laboratory to take part in an experiment that was going to ruin their lives.

The realisation of such an idea had spurred Graham's enthusiasm, and he made up his mind to go. This time he would see it through, he couldn't live the rest of his life without finding out whether they were like him or not. Whether he would be accepted as part of the group rather than standing on the side-lines.

"Thank you Dr. Wainright." Graham beamed up at her, ignoring the concerned look on her face. "You're right. I will go to London and meet them."

"I'm happy to hear that, Graham. Would you like to cut today"'s session a little short and go now?"

Graham glanced at the clock, he'd only be losing fifteen minutes, but it would mean he could make it on the next train into London.

"Yes please, if that's ok." He rose from his chair and shook Dr. Wainright's hand. "I'll see you next time."

"I look forward to hearing about your trip." She smiled back at him, seeing him to her office door. Waving to her and her secretary, Graham left the office with a spring in his step. Today was going to be a good day, he could feel it.

Imogen Chidwick

Imogen had found an empty seat in the quiet zone on the train. Away from all the noise of the other passengers trying to get into London, this was a haven. She didn't want to hear about their lives, and who had done what. Nor did she want to listen to small children demanding sweeties or have to avoid them as they ran around the train, taunting parents that had given up caring a few stops ago.

The quiet carriage was almost empty, so she'd been free to sit wherever she liked rather than next to someone else. Sitting beside someone else made it awkward to read a book because you had to be careful not to elbow them. Plus, books always enticed people to ask you about them, even though that was always the last thing you wanted.

Reclining in her seat a little, Imogen pulled her book from her bag, opened it at the bookmark and dove in. She was reading The Picture of Dorian Gray for the fifth time, and still enjoyed it as much as she had the first.

Slipping into the world of fiction, Imogen was vaguely aware of the train stopping at the next station. London was the last stop, so she didn't bother to look up. As the train pulled away again, she heard the swoosh of the carriage doors behind her and the low rumbling of someone pulling a suitcase on wheels.

As the newcomer approached, Imogen could hear music. It was muffled by headphones, but it must have been loud for her to be able to hear it as well. She glanced up from her book as the person - it was a tall, black woman with sleek black hair pulled back from her face - strolled past where she was sat.

For a moment their eyes met, and Imogen felt a sense of familiarity. Had she seen this woman before? The woman had stopped as well and was looking at Imogen with a curious expression. She fumbled in her pocket for a moment and the music stopped. The silence that followed was almost deafening until she pulled back her headphones and asked;

"Are you Imogen?"

Imogen blinked at her. So she had met this person before. "Yes..."

"I'm Bonnie."

"Okay.." Imogen still had no idea where she knew this Bonnie person from.

Bonnie clicked her tongue and rolled her eyes. Reaching into her pocket, she pulled out a single blue glove.

It clicked then, finally. "Oh! Of course! It's so nice to meet you."

"I didn't think I'd be running into anyone on the train, what a coincidence! Are you excited about meeting everyone else? I sure am!"

Imogen smiled as Bonnie rambled on, she definitely liked the sound of her own voice.

"Yes, it'll be nice to finally get to see everyone in person, rather than through the internet."

"Definitely," Bonnie nodded emphatically. "When we meet up, we'll all be able to see how many of us posted a fake picture."

Imogen smiled and agreed, marking her place and putting her book back into her bag. She probably wouldn't get to read much more of it with Bonnie around. At least there were only a couple more stops to go and It'd be nice to go into this knowing at least one other person.

Dominic Harper

Dom sat outside the aquarium waiting for the others to arrive. He'd accidentally arrived almost an hour early and was left with nothing to do but wait around. Normally he would have surfed the internet while he waited, but he'd been unable to find a connection strong enough to use outside of the aquarium.

As he sat against the barrier that bordered the Thames, strumming the fingers of his gloved hand on his bag, he remembered that he needed up update his e-diary. He'd started it when he'd found out about the experiment thinking that one day it could be a valuable source of information.

Unzipping the front compartment of his messenger bag, Dom pulled out a sleek, black laptop and set it in front of him. He opened it and waited patiently while it loaded up before opening a new document, knowing he could copy it over to the rest of his diary later when he had internet access.

20th July 2018

11:45 The meet up is scheduled for 12:00. I am the first to arrive at the Aquarium, and the others aren't due for another fifteen minutes. Hopefully they will all be on time.

Weather is good. Hardly any clouds in the sky, and there is a cool breeze keeping the temperature from being overbearing. Forecast is sun all day.

I'm starting to feel nervous about meeting the others. I'm having doubts about how well I'll fit in with them, and whether they will like me. In one of these girls resides the partner to my implant. I am curious to see how the proximity of the two implants will affect us, and whether I will be able to tell which girl is my partner.

The aquarium looks busy today because of the summer holidays. This should provide ample opportunity to talk to each other about the experiment without arousing suspicion.

11:50 I see a male approaching wearing a single blue glove. He is tall; roughly 6 feet. He has black hair combed neatly, and green eyes. I believe it is Aaron. Confirmation is needed, however. I'm going to attempt a greeting.

11:51 Identity is confirmed. Aaron Maysh (#01) has arrived. He looks nervous.

11:54 Imogen Chidwick (#09) and Bonnie Kinsella (#02) have now joined us. They arrived together after meeting on the train. Imogen seems very shy, and Bonnie very outspoken.

11:54 Aaron Maysh, Bonnie Kinsella, Dominic Harper and Imogen Chidwick are currently at the aquarium. We are still waiting for the other six to arrive. Everyone seems to be getting along well. I still don't know whether either of these are my partner or not.

11:55 Jennifer Dillon (#10) has arrived.

11:57 Farrell Brennan (#06), Graham Ahern (#07), Ethan Foy (#05) and Helen Askew (#08) are now at the aquarium. We are waiting for Camilla Everett (#03) to arrive.

12:00 Still no sign of Camilla.

12:05 Still no sign of Camilla. Unfortunately, no-one has her contact number so we have to wait around.

12:13 Camilla (#03) has arrived. All ten of us are now at the aquarium. Everyone looks excited to see each other. Some people also look nervous. Still no indication as to which girl might be my partner.

12:15 Time to go in to the aquarium. More updates to follow.

Aaron Maysh

Aaron had never been to the Aquarium before and was excited to see how much it differed from the small aquariums he had visited in the past with his family. He could tell it would be different when he paid for his entry; he'd never been to an aquarium that cost so much! He'd been told by his parents that everything cost more in London, but he hadn't believed it until now.

When they had all purchased their tickets, the ten of them had a brief and unanimous vote to save the best thing for last; the sharks. For a while, the ten of them walked the aquarium in near silence that was only broken when someone commented on one of the weirder looking fish.

Aaron didn't like the silence, but he also couldn't think of anything to say to get the others talking. He had never been very good at that kind of socialising. Thankfully he didn't have to worry very long, however, because Bonnie and Camilla soon started chatting away loudly enough for everybody.

"Where did you get those shoes?" Cam asked, and Aaron thought he heard a collective groan ripple through the five guys present. As he drove the shopping conversation out of his mind, Aaron spotted a sign and nudged Dominic.

"Hey look, we could feed the rays!" He walked towards a large, tank that came up to his waist and peered in. There were dozens of rays gliding beneath the surface of the water, their brown backs shining under the artificial lights overhead. He was glad to see that Dominic had followed him, along with Jennifer, Helen and Ethan.

189

Across the tank, a keeper was holding a small child up so that they could reach into the tank and touch one of the rays. Aaron decided to give it a go himself, and leant over, slowly sinking his hand into the cold water.

"What are you doing?" Jenifer asked him. He opened his mouth to reply when a ray brushed against his outstretched fingers. It was cold, and he jumped, tugging his hand away with a yelp.

"What did it feel like?" Helen asked as Ethan and Dominic doubled over laughing at him.

"Slimy and cold." Aaron chuckled, he probably would have laughed as well if it had happened to one of the others. He was grateful though, when Helen stepped forwards and reached into the tank.

"Ewwww." She laughed, as one of the rays bumped against her fingertips. "You're right." She pulled her hand out and flicked the water towards the laughing boys. Camilla and Bonnie had realised that most of the others had wandered off now, and also came over to see what they were doing.

"I can't believe you're doing that." Bonnie grimaced when they found the four of them with their hands in the water stroking the rays.

"Why don't you try it?" Aaron smiled.

"With these nails?" Cam snorted, holding up what Aaron assumed to be a freshly manicured hand.

"I don't think so." Bonnie nodded her agreement. Camilla and Bonnie were very alike, and Aaron noticed that they seemed to have hit it off straight away, even though Bonnie had arrived with Imogen. Imogen didn't seem bothered by this in the slightest, she was a much quieter person than Bonnie, and was happy enough wandering along towards the back of the group. Other people tried to draw her into conversations every now and then, but she only gave short answers. Maybe she was just shy.

The people that Aaron had found it easiest to talk to so far were Dominic and Jennifer. Although neither of them liked that he used their full names and asked him to call them Dom and Jen whenever he forgot.

They chatted about random things; what they did, where they were from, what had happened when their parents had told them and everything in between.

It turned out that Dominic had known about his adoption for years and had already come to terms with it. The experiment though, he had only found out about when the others had. He wasn't very phased by this either, Aaron came to realise. Dom liked science and was more intrigued by the whole thing than anything.

He wanted to know how they had been chosen, what the implants were like, how they had affected him and numerous other things that Aaron had already forgotten.

Jen on the other hand, had freaked out like Aaron had. Her parents had tried very hard to keep the whole thing from her, but she had found out anyway. She was still angry with them, and Aaron made a note not to bring it up again.

As the rest of the aquarium passed by in a blur of colour and oddly shaped fish, Aaron tried to work his way around the whole group and introduce himself to everyone. He was very pleased to find that he liked them all. One of his biggest worries about coming to the meet was that none of them would get along and it would be a long, awkward afternoon. Luckily it had been quite the opposite.

When they neared the tunnel shaped like a blue whale skeleton, the group fell silent and peered at it.

"Looks creepy in there." Bonnie whispered to Cam, who nodded.

"What's the matter ladies?" Ethan laughed, "Scared? Come on Farrell, let's show 'em how it's done!" The two boys stepped forwards and disappeared into the dark tunnel.

Rolling their eyes, Bonnie and Cam followed them with the rest of the group in tow. It was much creepier inside the tunnel; the curved ceiling and walls were made of glass and they were surrounded by fish of all shapes and sizes including the main event - the sharks! Farrell and Ethan were nowhere to be seen.

"Maybe they got bored and went ahead." Helen shrugged, when Cam voiced her concern about the two boys.

"Well they could have waited!" Cam pouted. "Come on, Bon, let's go find them."

Aaron turned his attention to the giant tank that surrounded them as the two girls wandered off. The view was amazing! And Aaron watched in silent awe as a huge shark swam overhead, suddenly very aware that there was only a bit of glass separating them.

An ear-piercing shriek tore Aaron's attention away from the giant fish, and he rushed through the tunnel with the others. Ethan and Farrell were holding their sides and laughing loudly, as they approached, Ethan wiped a tear from his eye.

"What happened?" Dom asked.

"Those two idiots thought it would be funny to jump out at us as we came round the corner." Cam scowled.

"I think I've had enough of the aquarium now." Said Bonnie, "Let's go and grab some lunch instead." Without waiting for an answer, Bonnie and Cam strode off towards the exit with the others trailing behind them. Ethan and Farrell bought up the rear, still giggling to each other and mocking the two girls and their reaction.

Dr. Linden Ranford

Linden flinched as her phone rang and she quickly drew it out of her pocket to silence it. "Dr. Linden Ranford." She answered.

"It's Cole."

"Ah yes, are the preparations in place?"

David had taken her to one side a couple of days ago and told her that he wanted to activate the implants fully for a couple of minutes; ten at most. Not just perform the test they had initially discussed. He wanted see whether they worked properly before they were fully initiated in a couple of weeks' time. At the moment they were mostly dormant, to allow the subjects time to adjust to the idea that they were in an experiment.

"They are indeed." He replied, "Are they in a suitable environment?"

"Yes." Linden looked over at the group, they were currently all sat in a courtyard enjoying cold drinks and chatting with one another. They weren't alone either; there were at least a couple dozen other people crammed in there as well, with other people milling around them.

"Remind me again what's going to happen to them?" She asked as she watched one of the girls freak out when a wasp flew close to her.

"I'm going to activate the implants. This will start to release the hormones that control sexual attraction, but that's going to happen very slowly and they won't feel it for a couple of days at minimum. Activation will also cause the implants to beep. We installed sensors to allow the subjects to know when they are in range of their partner implants, the closer they are the more they will hear the beeping. Each subject should only be able to hear their own beep, and anyone viewing or nearby will hear nothing." David explained. "That's what I want you to watch out for now."

"Sounds hilarious." Linden grinned, the ten of them were sat very close together, and she knew exactly who was paired with who thanks to the photos she had printed off from the Soul Echo website. "And you want me to document my observations?"

"Yes. I look forward to reading them. I'll text you when I activate the implants and again when I deactivate them. Which should be at around half past."

"Right. I'll get ready."

"Bye." She heard David put down the phone on the other end and placed hers on the table in front of her beside her notebook and pen, so she'd be able to see his message.

She'd sent Juniper off to secure them rooms for the night at any available hotel she could find. Well, perhaps not any. She'd given her assistant strict instructions to find a decent one. With two beds. Because she was not sharing a bed with that duvet stealing assistant of hers ever again.

The text arrived as she was taking a sip of her drink and she very nearly choked in her hurry to turn it off.

Count to 10. D.

She locked her screen again and made sure she was sitting comfortably before picking
up her pen and paper and watching the ten intently.

Aaron Maysh

Aaron's feelings of unease had settled throughout the day. He'd travelled all this way to meet up with the others like him, afraid that no-one else would turn up, but they were all there, and they all seemed to be getting along fine.

Glancing around the group as they sat in the sunshine, he wondered again which of the girls he'd been paired with now that he'd actually met them all in person. As bad as it might be, he really hoped that he hadn't been paired with Cam. Who seemed to have her own ideas about Ethan anyway. Or Bonnie, who was a bit too boisterous and loud for his liking. Any of the other three would be fine though.

As he looked over at the other guys, his thoughts turned a little sour; what if the girl he was paired with didn't like him. He wasn't sporty like Ethan or Farrell, strong like Graham or even book smart like Dom. In fact, beside them he felt inferior, like the booby prize. Or it could be worse. What if the scientists had inserted the implants wrong; somehow gotten them mixed up and he ended up partnered with one of the guys? What would happen then?

Turning his head to listen to the conversation Jen, Imogen and Dom were having about a film they'd all seen recently, Aaron heard something beeping. It started off relatively quiet but grew progressively louder, reaching a point that was almost unbearable within seconds. What the hell was going on, was this a fire alarm?

Aaron jumped up from his seat and looked around, noticing that the others were doing the same - could they hear it too? Good. That meant he wasn't hearing things. They rose from their seats as well, joining him and Aaron took a step away before stopping.

No-one else had reacted at all. They were surrounded by thirty-odd people who were still going about their conversations as if nothing was happening. One or two turned to glance at the group as they all rose, but then turned back to whatever they'd been doing.

"Can you hear something?" Aaron practically shouted at Imogen. She turned to look at him with wide eyes.

"You can hear it, too? I thought it was a fire alarm at first, but no-one else is reacting."

Aaron nodded, and Dominic piped up, "The beeping?"

"So it's not just me?" Ethan added, wiggling a finger in his ear.

"Okay, so raise your hand if you can hear it." Cam announced, "So much easier than all of us repeating ourselves." All ten of them raised their hands, earning odd looks from the people sat on the tables closest to them.

"Can't you hear the beeping?" Ethan asked a couple sat at the next table. "There isn't a fire alarm going off or anything?" They shook their heads, looking up at Ethan as though he were crazy before rising from their seats and walking away quickly.

"Guys." Dom whispered, motioning for them all to come close. "I think this is just an us thing."

"You mean the things in our heads are doing this?" Bonnie asked.

"I think so, yes."

"Why?"

"I have no idea. If there was internet access here, I could try and look it up."

"Well I hope it shuts up soon," Cam complained, "Or it's going to give me a migraine."

"Maybe we should go somewhere a little less public?" Helen suggested.

"If we go anywhere too quiet, then the beeping will seem louder." Jen frowned.

"Well, why don't we find some Wi-Fi? That way Dom can try and find out what the hell is going on with our heads."

"I like that idea." Cam nodded, "The sooner we figure out how to shut these things up the better." Everyone murmured in general agreement and started to gather their things.

"Oh, hang on." Jennifer said, her cheeks flushing a little, "I just need to use the bathroom."

"Me too, actually." Imogen nodded. "Let's go."

"Okay, we'll wait over there." Cam pointed to the little gate leading out of the courtyard. As the nine of them moved towards the gate, Aaron's beeping started to diminish. He looked up, and was going to ask everyone else when he saw the expressions on their faces. Their beeps were obviously still going strong and he decided not to say anything for fear that his implant really was defective.

They milled around while they waited for Jen and Imogen to come back and Aaron basked in the almost quiet of his mind. Hopefully the implant would stop beeping at him altogether. No such luck. The beeping soon returned to its original volume.

"Okay we're ready." Jen announced from beside him as she approached with Imogen. He looked at her with a puzzled expression, before moving away and standing on the other side of the group. When he moved away from Jen and Imogen, his beeping got quieter! Jen was watching what he was doing and took a few steps towards him. Before she had closed even half the distance, the beeping in Aaron's head grew louder and faster. Her eyes opened wide and he was instantly relieved that it wasn't just his implant that was playing up. He was not faulty.

A little confused, the two of them walked as far apart as possible as the group moved towards somewhere with internet access. Everyone was being quieter now, mulling in their own thoughts, so they didn't notice Aaron and Jen's strange behaviour. Or if they did, they didn't say anything.

Dominic Harper

Dom grumbled to himself as they traipsed along. All of the cafés and various places they had passed that had been wi-fi accessible so far were either packed, or you had to pay through the nose to use them.

They had stopped for a moment, resting on the rim of a large fountain when it finally happened. The beeping stopped! They had all looked up and glanced at each other questioningly.

"It stopped?" Cam asked.

"Yes!" Ethan grinned, punching the air enthusiastically.

Happy that the beeping was gone, Dom made a mental note to look it up later anyway. Perhaps he would email Dr. Hunter about it. He was almost positive that he'd read something about the beeps before though, but he couldn't quite place it. Had it been on the HSSE website? In the letter? It had to be from something connected with the experiment.

He didn't have the letter with him, but he was ninety-five percent sure that it hadn't been mentioned in there; He had read it enough after receiving it that the words were practically etched on his brain. It must have been on the website! But without internet access, he couldn't check.

"Earth to Dom?"

He blinked and almost shuffled backwards into the water fountain when he found Bonnie right in front of his face waving a hand and calling his name.

"Sorry, what?"

Bonnie tsked at him and sighed. "We were voting on what to do next..." She stood back and turned to face the others.

"Let's try that again. All those for going bowling."

Only four of them raised their hands.

"And all those for-"

"Ooh, look! There's a fair!" Cam interrupted, receiving a glare from Bonnie for doing so. "Let's go!" Everyone murmured their agreement, and Dom never found out what the second option had been. He was a little apprehensive about going, the only other time he'd been to a fair he'd been five and managed to get lost. This had resulted in him having to wait with a giant clown while an announcement was put out for his parents to find him. He'd realised later on that the clown had only seemed giant because he was five, but he had been a little nervous about fairs and clowns since then.

Dr. Linden Ranford

The ten subjects had moved out of the courtyard, and Linden dragged her assistant along after them.

"We need to find out where they're going." She hissed, before realising that Juniper wasn't even walking beside her anymore. Confused, she turned around until she finally spotted her leaning over a sandwich board.

"What the hell are you doing?" Linden asked, as her assistant stood up and beamed at her.

"I know where they went!" Juniper practically bounced over to her and Linden dreaded the next words to come out of her mouth. "They've gone to the fair!"

When they got to the fair it was packed but considering their reason for being there the more people the better. At first Linden considered splitting up but letting Juniper loose in an environment like this would be a huge mistake. She had little tolerance for sugar, and just the smell of the candy floss itself might be enough to send her off the wall.

"Where do you think we should look first?" She asked, narrowing her eyes as she saw Juniper edging towards a stall laden with sweets.

"I want to go on everything!" Juniper replied rather unhelpfully. Linden shook her head and moved on, keeping her sharp eyes peeled for any sign of the ten. She tried to think back to when she had been younger, where would she have headed to first? What would they have wanted to get out of the way in order to be able to do other things? It didn't work, Linden hadn't really been the fair-going type of teenager.

Looking around, she saw that most of the stalls were the kinds where you win prizes and had to carry the silly, over-sized toys around all evening. They were probably the last place people would want to go.

If the people that attended fairs had even a modicum of common sense, then they would head for the bigger rides first, then head for some food. After that it would make sense to tackle the smaller things, such as the waltzes. They couldn't have arrived here that much sooner than she and Juniper had, so surely, they'd be at the back somewhere.

Realising she had not heard the incessant chattering of her assistant for a little while, Linden turned. She sighed and resisted the urge to hit herself in the face. Juniper was happily eating candy floss.

"Want 'um?" Juniper asked through a mouthful of pink fluff.

"No."

"Ooh!" Juniper squealed.

"What now?"

"I just saw one of them!" She pointed enthusiastically to the right, nearly taking someone's eye out. Linden looked, but she couldn't see any of them.

"Are you sure?"

Instead of replying, Juniper took Linden's hand and pulled her along behind her. Sure enough, her sugar addled assistant had been right. The ten of them were waiting to go on the ghost train.

"Can we go on?"

"No, we might lose them."

Juniper pouted.

"Fine. You may go on it, but I'm going to wait out here." With a happy squeal, Juniper ran off to join the back of the line. Linden watched with a sinking stomach as Juniper managed to manoeuvre herself into a space where she would be right next to one of the subjects. If she did anything stupid, their cover would be blown.

The ghost train ride was two storeys high, and Linden could hear screams coming from inside. As they went along the top level, the cars would pop out onto a track where they were visible from the rest of the fair, and everyone could laugh at the riders as they were scared by the puppets that jumped out at them.

At the very end of the ride sat a man in a gorilla suit. As each car popped out at the end and the passengers thought they were safe, he would move suddenly and yell at them. Linden couldn't help snickering as Juniper practically jumped into Graham's lap to get away from the masked menace.

Camilla Everett

Cam clung to Ethan's muscular arm as they got out of the ghost train carriage. She'd decided that out of all of them, Ethan was the boy that she wanted to be partnered with. From his reactions, he seemed to share her opinion and the two of them had spent a large part of the day flirting; their encounter in the aquarium earlier long forgotten.

But there was also Helen. Ethan had met her before everyone else during the summer while they were at a sports camp. He said that they were just friends, but Cam had her suspicions. If she wanted Ethan, she was going to have to fight for him.

"Ethan!" She trilled, pulling on his arm, "I bet you can't make the bell ring." She pointed at a fair game. It was called Feat of Strength! And you had to hit the panel at the bottom to make bell ring at the top. It was pretty lame, but it was the first thing she had seen and she wanted to draw Ethan's attention away from Helen and windsurfing and back to her.

"Just watch me." He grinned, rubbing his hands together and picking up the mallet. Cam threw a triumphant glare towards Helen, but if she noticed she didn't show it. Ethan raised the mallet above his head and bought it down with a grunt, striking the panel just off centre. The ball rose up the tower and struck the bell.

"Yes!" Ethan grinned, "Told you I could do it." The man at the stall passed him a stuffed bear, and he handed it to Cam.

"For me?"

"Of course."

"Thank you." Cam held the bear close to her chest. She really did hope that the two of them were implant partners. She had never felt like this with anyone before. In that moment, she resolved to find out whether they were, and if they weren't well... she would petition the scientists or something!

Jennifer Dillon

Jen was tired. It had been a long day, fun but exhausting. She slouched in her chair a little as they waited for their food to be served. When it had started to get dark they'd left the fair and decided that it was time to eat. Everybody had agreed wholeheartedly, and they had set off in search of somewhere nice to eat.

They'd ended up in a nice pub restaurant where they could lounge around and chat to each other as a group rather than in twos and threes as they had been doing for most of the day. Taking a long drink from her glass, Jen looked around the table. Almost everyone was smiling and talking to someone. She was glad that she had decided to come and meet with them today, even if it was going get her into a lot of trouble if her parents found out where she had actually been all day.

Graham, she noticed as she looked around the group, looked a little uncomfortable. He'd been the quietest out of all of them all day, and Jen wondered whether this was just because he was nervous, or because he was also doubting. In any case, she decided to try and draw him into a conversation.

"Have you enjoyed today, Graham?" She asked, turning to face him.

"Yes."

"Are you glad you came?"

"Yes."

Jen tried her hardest not to frown. She hated it when people made it so hard to have a conversation. She'd been about to try again but their food arrived and she forgot all about it as the smell of her gammon steak washed over her.

Out of the corner of her eye, she watched as Graham downed his pint and asked for another one. Out of the five boys, she sincerely hoped that Graham wasn't her partner. If he was, she wasn't sure what she would do. Shaking her head, she turned to the person beside her.

Aaron, she'd discovered, lived not far from where she did. In fact, by some strange coincidence, they had both ended up in the same hospital A&E a couple of weeks before when she had been hit by the car. Her collar bone had pretty much healed now and she'd been able to take her splint off just for today, but it still ached without painkillers. His accident hadn't been quite as serious as hers; he'd just managed to cut his thumb open with a sharp kitchen knife.

"So, which school did you go to?" She asked him, wondering whether they might have gone to the same one and not even realised it.

"Saint David's. It was a catholic school." So no then. "You?"

"I went to Nelson's."

"Would you like another drink?" He asked her as he finished off the last of his own cola.

"Oh, yes please." She smiled, making a mental note to buy him one back later on in the evening.

"Did you hear that guys!" Ethan boomed across the table. "It's Aaron's round!"

Graham Ahern

Raising his fourth pint to his mouth, Graham realised that he was starting to feel a little drunk. He'd hardly eaten anything all day due to nerves. Even though he'd kind of met them all online first, it hadn't helped at all and he'd been struggling with his anxiety all day.

Needless to say, it had been a huge shock to arrive at the train station and run into the boy he'd bullied for the past couple of years. He found out that his name was Farrell, and that he was also part of this experiment.

That was it, he couldn't take it anymore. All evening he'd watched the others having fun and socialising. Even Farrell, who'd been shooting him snide looks all night, was becoming more outgoing as he realised that Graham wasn't going to beat him up.

He wondered if Farrell had told the others about what he'd done, maybe that was why they were so happy to socialise and leave him out of it. That would probably explain it. Well he hoped they were all happy talking and laughing about him behind his back. Screw them. Looking around, he wasn't sure which of the girls was his partner, but they had all ignored him for the most part. Except for Jen. She seemed nice enough, but maybe that was all a lie as well.

After another look from Farrell, Graham lurched to his feet and ambled towards him.

"What do you want?" Farrell asked, backing away a little.

"I want you to stop looking at me like I'm a piece of shit you trod in."

"I haven't done anything to you! And I never did!"

"Do you two know each other?" Aaron asked.

Farrell turned towards the others, turning his back on Graham. That was a mistake.

"Yeah, Graham's the guy that's been kicking the shit out of me for the last couple of years because his own life is too fucked up for him to deal with!"

Wham! Graham raised his arm and swung his fist into Farrell's jaw, knocking him backwards into Ethan.

"Woah, dude chill out!" Ethan frowned, steadying Farrell. Everyone else seemed to have stepped forwards, filling the gap between the two of them.

"Yeah, leave him alone!" Bonnie growled.

"It aint got nothing to do with you!" Graham spat.

"You made it our business when you decided to beat on Farrell. We're meant to be a team here. In it together." Aaron told him. Ethan had stepped in front of Farrell now as well.

"Get out of my way." Graham grunted.

"No."

"Then you're all against me!" He took a step towards them and raised his fist again, making Helen flinch a little. Dom immediately stepped in front of her. Glaring at them all, Graham turned on his heel and fled the restaurant. On his way out he reached into his pocket and pulled out a bottle of pills. Anxiety medicine prescribed by his psychiatrist when he'd told her about his meet up with the others.

"You will probably need them." She had told him bluntly. "Meeting up with a big group of people can be a very daunting experience." He had scoffed at her then and told her that it was no big deal. As he left the noise of the restaurant behind, it gave his mind more room to speak out and it told him things that he didn't want to hear about. Especially not now, not after what had just happened with the others. They would probably not allow him back into the group now, not unless he begged and apologised to Farrell.

Your mum and dad only stayed together because they were contracted to.

They never wanted you. You're just some poor kid that was abandoned by his real parents. They didn't want you. They stuck you in that experiment. And now you've gone and blown it with what could quite possibly be the only people on the planet who understand the situation you are in.

They could have been your friends if you had let them. You could have changed yourself for the better, found yourself a future. But it's too late now, moron.

Too late.

You are worthless.

No-one likes you.

You are all alone.

Why are you still here?

Why don't you just give up already?

Graham paused, his breath hitching in his throat, and he whirled around, certain that he had heard footsteps behind him. Maybe someone had come after him? But there was nobody there. He scowled and dug his hand into his pocket, reaching for his pills again, but instead his hand curled around an idea.

Maybe he should just give up. He had nothing left to live for, nothing to gain by staying. It was decided then. The only thing left to do was to figure out how.

Less than five minutes later Graham found himself on top of the high wall that separated the back alleys and the main town centre. Standing tall, with his back to the town centre he had come from, he looked down into the back alleys. Even if he only hurt himself, no-one would find him for hours. At this time of night no one dared to venture down there.

Having taken all of the pills he had been given, Graham was feeling blissfully numb. As he was about to take a step off the ledge, he heard a strange noise behind him again. It was a shuffling noise and it sounded a lot closer this time. He tried to turn to see what it was, but he was too close to the edge.

Without even a cry for help, Graham fell sideways from the top of the wall.

Dr. Linden Ranford

Linden watched quietly from the shadows. She and her assistant Juniper had been monitoring the subjects all day. Hunter had tried to stop them, but he'd been outvoted and so here they were. Besides, what better to add to their research than observational notes. It was done with animals during science experiments, and humans were animals too, right?

The group had finally decided to get something to eat, much to Juniper's delight. She'd been complaining that she was hungry for the better part of two hours prior to this. The two of them had followed them into the restaurant and found a table close by so that they could observe. Nothing much had happened until #07 had attacked #06 and then run away. After informing her assistant to stay and observe what happened next with the group in the restaurant, Linden had taken off after Graham, curious as to what he would do next. Would he come back for another confrontation, or just go home.

She followed him carefully towards the darker streets that led to the back alleys, having to hide once or twice when her footsteps had been carelessly loud and Graham had turned almost spotting her. He had stopped for a long while at a railing, seemingly lost in his own thoughts. They couldn't have been good ones either, judging on what had happened next.

Graham had upended a pot full of pills into his mouth and choked them down, before discarding it and disappearing into the shadows. Linden had crept after him, stopping quickly to inspect and take notes on what kind of pills he'd just taken and by the time she found him, he was on top of a wall. Lord knows how he had managed to get up there, but if he fell the drop was more than enough to kill him. Idiot.

Unless that was his intention. In which case, should she interfere and stop him from killing himself, or should she step back and observe. Just recording the outcome as she did with any other experiment she took part in.

She still hadn't decided when her assistant Juniper appeared out of nowhere beside her, her bushy hair wild and her cheeks flushed. Linden quickly clamped a hand over her mouth before she could speak and looked back up at the wall just in time to see Graham look around, startled by the noise, and fall from the wall, disappearing on the other side.

"Was that- Did he just-" Juniper rambled. Linden nodded with an exasperated sigh.

"Yes, that was #07. I think you might have just scared him off the wall."

Juniper's watery blue eyes opened wide and she clapped her own hand to her mouth this time.

"Calm down, I believe he was attempting suicide anyway." Linden told her, before she started hyperventilating or something.

"That doesn't make it any better! Why would he want to kill himself?"

"How the hell should I know? It's not as if we had a huge heart to heart before he overdosed and climbed up there." Linden waved her arm towards the wall dramatically. "From what I read on the forums, he had a dysfunctional home life. Perhaps what happened in the restaurant with the others drove him to extremes. Didn't his medical records also say that he was seeing a psychiatrist?"

Without waiting for Juniper to reply, Linden stalked out from the shadows. After failing to try and prevent Graham from killing himself, the least she could do was check whether he had succeeded or not.

"Juniper!" She called back to her assistant, who crept towards the other side of the wall but didn't dare look. "You had better call the police."

"Is he dead?"

"If he weren't I would have recommended an ambulance."

Juniper squeaked and Linden turned back to find her peeking around the wall, looking at Graham's contorted body. She'd never seen a dead body before, but her curiosity must have gotten the better of her. She vanished again, and Linden heard her on the phone. At least she hadn't vomited.

Standing over the body, being careful not to step in anything, Linden quickly, and rather morbidly, took notes on what she saw. He'd definitely broken his neck when he landed.

"The police are on their way, we should leave now." Juniper whispered, the sound of her footsteps indicating that she had joined Linden beside the body.

"Yes, Let's go back to the others."

"About that."

"What's happened?"

"They left the restaurant. That's what I came to find you. I managed to find out which hotel they were staying in before they left though."

Linden nodded, deep in thought. Hunter wasn't going to be happy that one of the subjects had killed themselves, but it was hardly her fault. He'd just have to deal with it. It was an unexpected outcome and would prove an intriguing one. What would the girl half of this pairing do when she realised her implant partner had died?

Speaking of the implant... Should she just leave the implant in Graham's body to be removed by a coroner later on or should she take it out? With the police already on their way, there was no time to phone Cole and ask his opinion, and she couldn't trust that the lab had any coroners that could intercept the body. No. The only way to ensure the safety of the implant would be to remove it herself.

"What the heck are you doing?" Juniper asked as Linden knelt beside the body.

"I need to retrieve the implant."

"But the police are coming!"

"I know that, I'll be quick. Go get that pill bottle and put it somewhere closer to the wall. We need to make it more obvious it was a suicide."

"Remember not to touch it with your fingers!" Linden called after her assistant as she moved away to retrieve the bottle. Juniper mumbled something, but if it was protests Linden couldn't hear them enough to care.

Delving into her bag, she looked for something she could cut with. Scissors? No they probably wouldn't work. Pen knife? Maybe. Then she found her first aid kit.

Perfect! She thought, pulling the small tin out of the bag, she always carried a small surgical blade around in there, just in case. There were no gloves unfortunately, so she would have to trust that the fact that she knew the exact location of the implant would lower the chances of her leaving behind a viable fingerprint on his skin. Not that she thought about that kind of thing... Often.

The sound of sirens started to fill the air, and Linden tried her hardest to keep her hand steady. Thankfully, the incision would be in the hairline, so it was quite possible that it could be overlooked, especially with the obvious broken neck. She had almost finished cutting when a clattering behind her made her jump.

"What was that?" She demanded.

"Nothing. I just dropped my bag. And some pens."

"Well you damned well better pick them up!" Linden snapped. She knew that her assistant had a thing for stationary and often carried around an army of pens, and that was the last thing they needed to leave behind. At least half of the damned things had been pilfered from the labs and were monogrammed with the Hunter and Sampson Science Enterprises brand.

"Gotcha!" Linden cried, as she pried the implant loose. Carefully placing it inside her first aid tin, she straightened up, made sure she had not left anything behind and stepped away from the body. Spotting a broken beer bottle nearby, she kicked it towards Graham and nudged a shard near his neck with the toe of her boot. There.

"Have you picked everything up?" She asked Juniper.

"Yes."

"Good. Let's get out of here." The two of them vanished into the back alleys moments before the streets flashed blue and red with the lights of a police car, their hearts pounding a thousand beats a minute and praying that everything would be okay.

To be continued...

31628793R00127

Printed in Great Britain
by Amazon